I0625112

VAMP REVEALED

SILVER DAGGER SISTERHOOD

KB ANNE

Copyright © SEPTEMBER 2022 by KB Anne

All rights reserved.

No part of this book may be reproduced in any form or by any electronic or mechanical means, including information storage and retrieval systems, without written permission from the author, except for the use of brief quotations in a book review.

This is a work of fiction. Names, characters, organizations, places, events, and incidents are either products of the author's imagination or are used fictiously.

No part of this book may be reproduced or stored in a retrieval system, or transmitted in any form or by any means, electronic, mechanical, photocopying, recording, or otherwise, without express written permission of the publisher.

Published by Gripping Tales, LLC, Pennsylvania.

Cover Design by Anika Willmans, Ravenborn Covers

Editorial Services by Laura Parnum, Laura Parnum Books

ISBN: 978-1-956915-13-6

For my Family,
Thank you for believing in me.
—Kim

CHAPTER
ONE

ez

THE SEXY FOOTBALL player sporting muscles for miles prowled toward me.

Sometimes, it was almost too easy.

"Hellooo, you," I purred.

He winked as he split the distance between us. "How *you* doing?"

I inwardly winced. Quarterback was yummy, I'd give him that, but using that cheesy Joey Tribbiani pickup line minutes after breaking up with my sister proved he wasn't worthy of her or anyone else for that matter. If he had fallen to his knees, flailing his arms up and down screaming, "I'm not worthy. I'm not worthy," I might have let him live, but the sight of my sister's tear-stained face as I watched from outside her bedroom window fueled my rage instead.

Yes, Quarterback would get exactly what was coming to him.

He wrapped his hands around my hips as if we were lovers. Far too familiar given he'd just broken up with my sister. Granted, he didn't know we were related. No one did. And if there hadn't been a familial connection, I might have given him a toss in the sack. See if he lit me up like his Friday-night scoreboard.

I grabbed the sides of his face, my human nails digging into his cheeks. He grinned.

"You like it rough, don't you? Want to blow me first?"

Oh, why did so many of the pretty ones have to be so stupid?

"I'm not here to blow you or hump you. I'm here to kill you."

He jerked away. Quarterback was strong, but I was stronger. Fear shot off him, putting a sour taste in my mouth. I'd never understand vamps who got off on the taste of fear, but then, they were often the ones who wound up with a silver stake through the heart.

I stared with intensity into his mud-brown eyes. "Quarterback, you don't need to be scared. Just relax and let Dez take care of you."

His pupils dilated in submission. "My name is Derrick, but I'm not the quarterback. I'm the running back."

Attention seeking even under my compellation.

"Quarterback, I don't care what position you play on the field or in the sack, and that's not a play on words about sacking the quarterback. Now, hold still, and I'll do the rest. Understand?"

He nodded.

I patted his cheek. "That's a good boy. Quarterback, I don't appreciate you dumping my sister."

His pupils pulsed as the realization lifted the compellation. "Cynda's your sister?"

I smiled at him as I stared, pulling him back into obeisance. "Yes, she is, and you broke her heart. Why did you dump her?"

His pupils dilated again. "I wanted to fuck around when I got to college."

"Along with the first woman you saw after breaking up with her?"

He shifted closer, his hard cock pressing against my leg. "Yes."

"Quarterback, I want to let you in on a little secret."

His lips dipped toward mine. "What?"

I opened my mouth, revealing fangs. His eyes widened, but he stayed calm like an obedient little quarterback.

"Life's full of disappointment."

And I bit into his neck.

CHAPTER
TWO

yn

I SPLASHED cold water on my face, trying to bring down the puffiness. My parents didn't need to witness my shame at Derrick breaking up with me. They'd twist our breakup into a shortcoming of mine, but it had absolutely nothing to do with me and absolutely everything to do with Derrick.

Wanting to end things before leaving for college.

Opening our horizons to new opportunities.

Staying in touch.

What a load of crap.

I wasn't an idiot. Derrick needed constant stroking (and I don't mean his ego), and if he couldn't get it from me, he'd get it from someone else. Everyone else.

I splashed my face some more. I didn't want to begin the next chapter of my life sad and broken. I stared at

4

myself in the mirror. I was sad and broken. And used. And an idiot.

When he had shown up at my door last night with that mischievous look in his eye, I knew he wanted sex. He always wanted sex. He pawed at me the second we entered my bedroom. Then he changed tactics and went for his shorts, yanking them to his knees as he shoved my head down to suck him without even so much as a "Hello."

I served as his obedient little girlfriend, all too used to his greeting.

He shot his load in my mouth suddenly and without warning, much faster than he'd ever done before. As I gagged, debating whether I should spit or swallow, he split ties and was out the door, leaving me sad, broken, and used.

I splashed more water on my face. I'd been an idiot to stay with him as long as I had, but my parents would have disowned me if I expressed any doubts about Derrick. They adored him, thinking I'd won the boyfriend lottery with the school's star running back. They loved him way more than they loved me. They were devastated when he didn't choose to go to West U with me, opting to stay closer to home on the eastern side of Kentucky at a college with a better football team. Their only consolation was that they could watch his games in person.

Rah. Rah.

Knock. Knock.

"Yes?"

"Cynda, we're leaving for work . . ." Mom said, her words trailing off as if she didn't really care whether or not she saw me before I left for West U. But the thing was, I wanted to see my parents one last time before heading off to college.

"One second." I grabbed a towel and patted my face, looking in the mirror again. The puffiness had gone down, but there was no hiding the emotional toll last night had taken on me.

I took a few deep inhalations to calm myself. All those years in the before-school Mindfulness program had taught me how to steady myself. It was the only way I got through high school. The only way I dealt with my disappointed absentee parents. The only way I'd get through the long drive to college by myself when my roommates all had either their mom or dad or both coming along to help them unload their stuff, decorate the room, and give them one last tearful hug goodbye before driving away.

Don't go there, Cynda.

I breathed in and out of my nose again and walked down the hall.

"Good morning!" I smiled, acting far more cheerful than I actually felt. Fake it till you make it, right?

My dad peeked over the morning paper clutched in his hands, his briefcase already packed and set on the dining room table next to him, leisurely waiting for Mom to snap her fingers for him to jump to attention. "Good morning, Cynda. Have a safe trip today."

Mom handed me a wad of cash and a credit card. "Yes, Cynda, remember to tip anyone who helps you unload."

I shoved the money and the card in my pocket. "Thanks, I think everyone will be busy helping their own kids move in."

Mom glared at me. "Now, Cynda, we've gone over this. Stan and I are too busy at work to take an entire day to move you in."

"But you own the firm . . ."

The largest law office in town, and they couldn't take

one day to help move their only daughter in. But god forbid Mom reacted to a Botox injection. She took a week off every three months "just in case."

Dad bunched up the paper and shoved it under his arm as he stood up. "Cynda, you know we've got a big case coming up."

It took everything in me not to roll my eyes. They always had a big case coming up. There was a reason we were the only family on our street with local newspaper delivery. The neighbors called my parents ambulance chasers behind their backs—until, of course, they needed to enlist their services.

I nodded, swallowing the lump in my throat. My parents didn't respond to emotional reactions. They wanted a cohesive argument loaded with facts. But I was still reeling from Derrick's breakup combined with the nervous knot in my stomach about leaving home. I couldn't form one coherent sentence let alone an entire argument. The slightest provocation would send me spiraling into another breakdown.

He patted my shoulder. "Drive safely, and we'll see you at Thanksgiving."

"Thanksgiving? You aren't coming for parents' weekend?"

Mom pointed her finger at me. "Now, Cynda, we talked about this. You need a clean break from us."

In other words, *We need a clean break from you*.

"And if something comes up and you can't make it for Thanksgiving, we will see you at Christmas," she added.

"Christmas?" I cried out, forgetting myself.

They frowned at me as if I were an opposing witness. I pushed down my emotions, not wanting to further disappoint them before they left.

"Okay."

"Well, good luck." Dad patted my back before heading for the door.

"Thanks."

"You'll do well." Mom gave me a small smile as she turned to leave.

"Wait." I rushed after her and threw my arms around her, desperate for one hug before they left.

She stiffened, never one for tenderness even when her only daughter was leaving for college. She kept her arms at her sides, but I didn't care. I squeezed her tight.

"That's enough."

I broke away and she straightened her suit. Her face remained as emotionally removed as it had always been these last ten years. So different from the loving, doting parents from the first eight years of my life. I blew out the eight candles on my birthday cake, and I became a major disappointment. I didn't understand what I'd done, but even still, they were my parents and I loved them.

"Goodbye," she said, pulling the door closed behind her.

"Goodbye," I called out, my voice shaking. As soon as the door clicked shut, I collapsed to the floor. Sad, broken, and used.

I cried for the loss of my parents. I cried for the loss of my boyfriend. I cried for the loss of my perfect life that had somehow gone to shit.

I cried until I didn't think I had any more tears to shed. Then I cried some more. And I would have stayed in that curled-up ball all day if my phone alarm hadn't broken me out of my pity party.

I clicked off the alarm, tempted to hit the snooze, but what would seven more minutes give me? I had a six-hour drive ahead of me. No reason to waste all my tears in a house where no one cared about my welfare when there was a perfectly good car to cry in, a car that never let me down. Of course, it couldn't hug back or dry my tears, but it was the closest thing I had to a friend. And I wanted to get to West U and unpack before nightfall. The night scared me.

I swiped away the last of my tears and pushed myself off the hardwood floor. I grabbed the laundry basket containing the last few things I needed from the foyer and left without looking back, shutting the front door behind me. Of course, I turned back to lock it. God forbid the house get burglarized the day I left for college—my parents would never speak to me again.

My chest heaved with another sob. I shook my head. Nope, no more pity parties, at least not until I got on the road.

I sighed with relief when I saw my car as I walked down the pathway. Dependable, reliable, and always took me where I wanted to go. The Prius, Pri for short, was a Sweet Sixteen present from my parents. Well, it was Mom's old prized Prius, but still, it was now mine. Getting my driver's license cut one of the final strings of their parental obligation. They went out to a fancy dinner the day I passed my test.

Another sob ripped through me.

Cynda, don't go there. Not yet.

I opened the back door and placed the laundry basket behind the front passenger seat. I wanted easy access to the granola bars and water bottles for my long ride but didn't want the basket tipping over in the front passenger seat, or worse, obstructing the shifter during my drive. With a full tank of gas, I didn't plan on stopping until I got to West U.

As I straightened, the hair on the back of my neck stood on end. The strangest feeling that I was being watched came over me. I slowly turned around, wishing I had my pepper spray.

"Hello, Sister," a tall woman with long raven hair said. "Long time no see."

From her black leather pants to her black tank top down to her scuffed black combat boots, this woman reeked of danger.

"Who are you?" I backpedaled away from her and rounded the front of the car, debating the merits of diving into the driver's seat and fleeing or racing back into the house and locking the door behind me.

Her purple eyes watched me, her pupils pulsing. I could feel myself leaning toward her.

"That hurts, Cyn. I'm your sister. Your long-lost sister."

A tiny thread pulled at my brain, telling me not to run, to listen to what this woman had to say.

"I don't have a sister. I'm an only child."

But as the words left my mouth, they felt false.

She raised an eyebrow, and her lips transformed into a devilish grin. "Oh, Cyn, I'm your sister, and those assholes aren't your parents. You've been fed a punch bowl of Kool-Aid since the day you were born."

My control slipped away from me, and I would have done anything to get it back. I fought against my inner desire to listen to her. "It's Cynda."

She stepped toward me. I wanted to back away, but I couldn't.

"Cynda, Cyn, Sister, it's all the same to me." Her purple eyes pulsed in and out as she watched me. That thread reformed, stronger than before, more determined to take hold. I latched on to the one piece of information that almost made sense, that somehow justified my parents' apparent lack of affection for me.

"What do you mean they aren't my parents?"

She glanced at her watch. "We're running out of time. I'd like to get going soon in case we have any delays."

"Delays? Is there construction on the highway? Google Maps didn't highlight any problems along the way to West U."

She appeared in front of me. "Sis, you are so cute. You're not going to West U."

I tugged at the thread tying me to her, but it held strong. "What do you mean?"

"We're going someplace better."

I tilted my head. "Better?"

"Much better. But in order to go there, I need to force the Change in you."

I didn't like the sound of that.

"What's that supposed to mean?"

"Sister, you and I are Sempiternals."

The word rang a bell in my head, like, *Ding, ding, ding! We have a winner!*

"What is that?"

She raised her hands as if she wanted to put them on me. "May I?"

"Yes," I said, not believing my answer. That I'd told this woman, this stranger who claimed she was my sister, that she could touch me. What was wrong with me?

She wrapped her fingers around my shoulders, her purple eyes never leaving mine. "We are from an ancient race known for immense power. Speed. Incredible hearing. Gorgeous looks. Extreme intelligence. Along with dozens of other abilities."

"Okay . . ." Something about this woman made me brave. Brazen even. She made me want to fight her.

"And if I don't take you now, the Children of the Sun will find you and kill you dead."

I blinked, not believing her claims. That she was my sister *or* that someone wanted to kill me. Sure, people didn't seem to like me, and clearly Derrick and my parents didn't want me around, but they didn't want me dead. "Are you sure?"

"Positive."

"Why would someone want to kill me?"

"Because you're a Sempiternal from a long, distinguished line of the original families."

"Original what?"

She opened her mouth, revealing two long white fangs. "Vampires."

CHAPTER

THREE

ez

MY SISTER TOOK the vampire reveal well, if "well" meant she passed out cold. Lucky for her I've got fast reflexes. I caught her and stuffed her into the passenger seat of the car. As I closed the door, I surveyed the neighborhood to make sure there weren't any nosy neighbors with memories that needed wiping. Couldn't have the police chasing after me for kidnapping Little Sis before I hit the boundary.

Not a soul for as far as I could see. I couldn't have created a better situation if I'd wanted to. And when I'd dumped Quarterback down that steep ravine, his big body had caused a mini avalanche. Not a living soul would find him. A giant smile spread across my face. The elements had aligned well for me this past week, first, with a solid lead on Cynda's location, and then when the guy who'd caused her grief stumbled in my direction and I showed him exactly what happens to douchebags who mess with my sister.

And let me tell you, his body was the only thing that was big. Guess he made up for his small dick by being an asshole to Cynda. Forcing her to swallow him whole and then not offering any satisfaction in return *and* breaking up with her? I had given him a far cleaner death than he deserved.

Her adoptive parents were horrible people too, perking up whenever Quarterback came to visit but ignoring their adopted daughter like she was some asshole who'd wandered into their living room. Unfortunately they held high-profile positions. They couldn't disappear without an investigation in which Cynda would serve as the top suspect—an unhappy daughter desperately searching for a way to fit into the world she didn't belong in. I could, of course, wipe their memories of her existence, and someday maybe I would, but I wanted them to suffer. Miss her when she didn't check in tonight. Or at the very least wonder what had happened to her every time they passed by her bedroom.

Hours later I patted her red hair, smiling to myself. Little Sis was still out cold. With any luck, her lack of sleep last night after Quarterback dumped her combined with the Great Vamp Reveal would mean she'd stay asleep until we reached the boundary. Then I'd smash the car into a tree, and her new life could begin. Cyn would soon discover the world she deserved to live in. Meet people who would praise her for her unique gifts, which had only just begun to manifest themselves. People who would honor her for her sacrifice of living with humans for almost two decades, how she had learned their ways and knew how to hide in the shadows. People who would cherish her as a Sempiternal from one of the original families.

Yes, Cynda would finally embrace her destiny.

"AHHHHHHHHHH!"

The scream broke me out of my come-to-goddess moment with my sister's unconscious form.

"Who are you, and why are you driving like a maniac?" she shrieked, having come to much faster than I would have liked.

I pressed my foot down on the gas. Her precious little Prius didn't possess much drive. Kinda like her ex.

"Just relax."

The tires squealed as I banked a tight corner. Loose rocks careened down the cliff. Her fear endorphins filled the car, and my mouth turned down. I really didn't understand how some supes got off on them.

"You're going to get us killed," she shrieked.

I turned to her and winked. "Exactly."

"You want to kill us? Are you insane?"

"Never confirmed, but who knows?"

She stared out the window, her fingers strumming against her seat belt. My guess, she was thinking about jumping out of the car, but I'd seen enough of her this past week to know she always chose the safe route. The path of least resistance. She never fought against Quarterback or her parents when they deserved it. But she'd find her voice at the Academy. I was sure of it. After all, she was a Wickershim.

I swerved again, getting close to the cliff edge. My sister's presence distracted me. But I couldn't get her killed until we reached the boundary. Before then, any civilian could pick us up, and when she came to, thirsting for blood, she'd leave a trail of bodies behind. That was a lot more complicated of a cleanup. I was already risking severe punishment by forcing Cyn's Change early, interfering with the natural cycles. If I caused extra deaths, an Elitest would serve justice with a silver dagger to my heart.

"You ought to thank me," I said.

She grunted, crossing her arms. "Explain why?"

"Would you rather me kill you and bring you back to life or have one of the Children of the Sun kill you with a stake to the heart and you stay dead?"

Annoyance replaced her fear. "Why would a bunch of strangers want to kill me?"

The car slowed as I eased my foot off the pedal. "Can you just thank me for allowing you early entrance into the most prestigious academy in the world and just be done with it?"

"What academy?"

She sounded interested. Good. She'd love it there. That curiosity would get her through Silverwood Prison faster.

A flash of light caught my attention in the rearview mirror. Car headlights were coming in fast. Much faster than just a random car driving on the road at night. I closed my eyes for one brief second and focused on the driver. Her corrupted energy signature left little doubt she was a member of the Children of the Sun. I could just envision her red lipsticked lips.

"Shit, we've got company. I'll explain later. Just hold on. Actually,"—I leaned over and unbuckled her seat belt—"don't, but try not to get yourself killed before I lose them, okay?"

Cyn peeked over her shoulder and saw the approaching headlights. "Are you sure they're really chasing us? They seem harmless."

"So does a basilisk before it strikes."

Suddenly the car slammed into our bumper, sending Cyn into the front windshield. I yanked her back into her seat.

"Shit. Maybe I shouldn't have unbuckled you yet."

"You think?" She clutched her forehead, buckling herself back up, which was probably a good idea given the two red-lipped bitches chasing us. How the hell had they found us? I'd only gotten the lead on Cyn's where-abouts last week, and I hadn't told anyone about it. Gage was the only other person who knew, and we'd thanked each other with multiple orgasms, so the snitch wasn't him.

His source then? But that didn't make sense.

Were they after me then? I always covered my tracks. Admittedly killing the quarterback was impulsive, but it was too sweet an opportunity to pass up. But the rockslide had covered his body. Unless of course . . . Shit. I slammed the steering wheel with my fist. The Children of the Sun had a recruiting station close to Cyn's town. It was one of the deciding factors why I was taking her before she changed. That and I wanted her close after Dad's death. I bet they'd sunk their little manicured nails into big, muscular Quarterback. He was their type. Strong and stupid with anger management issues. He must have had a tracker.

Cyn pulled her hand from her head. "I'm bleeding. I'm definitely bleeding. We need to get some bandages. Oh, wait, I packed some."

My mouth twitched at the sight of the blood. I'd feasted last night on Quarterback's energy, but the smell of blood still brought cravings. My fangs elongated on instinct. I forced them back in. I wasn't about to snack on my sister. She'd gone through enough already.

Speaking of which, she reached behind her seat, searching for something. A knife maybe?

"What are you doing?" I hit the gas. The car screamed in agony. If this piece of shit died before we hit the boundary, we were screwed.

"Found 'em," she shouted, pulling out a pack of gauze and a giant bandage.

"We're in the chase of our lives, and you're worried about a little cut on your head?"

"Yes."

"Yes?" I repeated. "You're a stodgy one. I hope you loosen up at the Academy, because you're a complete bore right now."

She tore off the bandage wrapper with her teeth and carefully applied it over the gauze. "Gee thanks, Sis. Love you too."

The corner of my lip curled as I stared out the windshield. Warm and fuzzy feelings filled my chest. I hadn't felt like this since . . . I couldn't remember when.

"That's the first time you've acknowledged we're sisters."

She leaned her head against the headrest, groaning. "Don't remind me. Blame it on blood loss, or maybe I have a concussion." She clutched her head. "Yes, I definitely have a concussion. Can you take me to a hospital for an evaluation?"

"Are you fucking kidding me right now?" Her priorities were out of whack. Hopefully almost two decades of living with mortals hadn't caused irreparable damage. "Oh goddess, what did I get myself into?"

"No need to curse," she muttered.

Bam! The Prius shuddered as our attackers slammed into us again. The sound of crumpling plastic, fiberglass, and metal rippled through the air. Stupid piece of shit car. I should have stolen one of her parents' Mercedes.

"If we can just get through the boundary," I whispered to myself, leaning forward. I could feel it calling to me. We were close, so close, but not there yet. As long as we crossed it, Cynda would survive.

She stared out the front windshield. "What boundary? It's pitch black out there. There's not a town or house in sight."

"That's what you think."

She gestured to the windshield. "That's what I know."

"Seeing isn't always believing. You'll learn—"

But I was cut off. The car got knocked into a tailspin, throwing its rear end around and spinning us to face the vamp-killing freaks and their red-lipsticked smiling faces before we spun again and again and again.

A shiver ran up my spine, vibrating through my entire body as we entered the boundary.

"We made it." I sighed in relief, unbuckling her seat belt. "Don't be scared, Cyn. Everything will be fine."

Screeching tires filled the air. The headlights illuminated a ginormous tree coming straight at us before we smashed headfirst into it.

CHAPTER
FOUR

ᵉᶻ

Twenty-one days since I turned my sister. Twenty-one days since we were thrown in this cell together. Twenty-one days since we met for the first time, and I introduced her to the supernatural world by wrapping her mom's prized Prius around a tree. Of course, I use the term "mom" lightly. Her real mom, my mom, disappeared after she gave birth to Baby Cynda, leaving Dad with an impossible choice—raise two girls on his own, or give one away so that at least one of us could have a chance at a "normal" life until the Change took place. He believed his precious little Cynda had won the parental lottery when he handed her off to a woman at the hospital wearing cashmere and pearls, who buckled her into the new infant car seat placed in the middle of the back row (the safest place in the car, in case you didn't know) and drove off with her.

I didn't get the pearls or the cashmere, unless the wicked scar on the side of my forehead counted as the Wickershim crown jewels. Fellow supes assumed I received it in battle, given my propensity for violence and my chosen vocation, which served as a much better story than the real one: Upon witnessing my little sister plop out of my mother's va-jay-jay and into my dad's arms, three-year-old me blacked out and smashed her head on the hard tile floor. Sometime between Dad cooing over my little sister in the nursery and the nurse discovering me lying in a pool of my own blood, Mom skipped out, but not before draining the doctor and three other nurses of every last drop of their blood.

Sempiternals—born vampires—pride ourselves on our incredible control over bloodlust. Well, once we successfully transition. There are, however, lapses during times of great duress, with Mom serving as Exhibit A-Z. So to prevent trails of bodies between the shopping mall and the local Uni-Mart, the Society locks up new vamps, Sempiternal and turned, plus those that fall off the blood wagon (or pretend to), here at Silverwood Prison.

"Preeeeety Dez, when are you going to let me wrap my hands around your preeeeeety little throat and eat you?" hissed the newbie demi-dragon shifter from the next cell.

Vampires weren't the only supes in this hellhole. All recently turned supernaturals are imprisoned until they prove they aren't a danger to humans and other supes. If they can't prove that by their twenty-fifth birthday, or if they're a repeat offender, Elitests terminate them. Quick and painless.

"Come on, preeeeety Dez. Just one mouthful," the shifter whined.

Twenty-five seemed too generous for some.

"Hands against the wall, vampire," a guard shouted at me from outside my cell. It was the scrumptious guardian angel who refused to tell me his real name no matter how many times I asked.

I stalked toward him. "Afraid of a couple of girls? We're completely harmless. It's that one you ought to worry about," I said, gesturing toward the demi-dragon.

The guardian angel knocked his billy club against the bars and set off a calming obedience spell. "You two are the most dangerous supes in the place. Now, hands up."

As pure Sempiternals and legacies to Silver Dagger Sisterhood, I agreed with his statement, but before I could argue—because of course I wanted to—his obedience spell took hold, forcing me to rest my hands high above my head against the closest wall.

"Why isn't your sister moving?"

"She's probably asleep, which I would be if you hadn't interrupted me." I nestled my boobs between the cell bars, hoping to befuddle his brain.

His gaze never left my face. Damn guardian angels and their virtues. He knocked his billy club against the bars a second time, this time chanting a rising spell.

I couldn't conduct magick—at least not yet—but when other kids had their own cashmere-sweater-wearing mommies take them to playdates and soccer practice, Dad was making me study every piece of supernatural lore in his possession, and as an Elitest, he owned an entire bunker full.

"Get back or I'll shoot the next one up your ass."

I winked at him. "Is that a promise?"

"Would you stop flirting with him, and leave me the fuck alone?"

I turned toward the bed. "Hey, Sis. Glad you're awake. We get released today. Tonight is our Induction Ceremony into Silverwood Academy."

SILVERWOOD ACADEMY
HAS THREE RULES:

1. Don't use magick on someone without their permission.
2. Don't bite anyone's neck, for nourishment or otherwise, without their expressed verbal consent.
3. Don't stab another classmate in the back. (Even if it's your own sister.)

FIVE

ᵉᶻ

MY SISTER PULLED at the tank top I let her borrow to cover her boobs. Then, realizing her efforts caused an exposed midriff, she yanked it down. She huffed in exasperation. "I'm not dressing like this. I look like a slut."

I narrowed my eyes at her. "Are you calling me a slut?"

Her pale green eyes widened. "Well, aren't you?"

I threw back my head and laughed. "Actually, you'd be correct in your assessment. I am a slut. We get our energy, our food, from other people. There are multiple ways in which to pull energy from them, but the most effective is intercourse." Over the past few weeks, I'd taken to messing with her at every opportunity. I mean, if she could survive twenty-one days in Silverwood Prison with me, she could certainly survive some teasing. Besides, half-truths and

26

exaggerations kept her on her toes—a helpful tool for a future hunter.

"You're telling me, in order to survive I need to have sex with people?"

It was almost too easy. My sister needed to abandon her prudish ways. She lacked experience, and I was just the person to unleash her. I pulled down my red tank top to ensure ample breast reveal, demonstrating to my sister exactly how a tank top should be worn. "Sex with multiple people is the most effective."

She gasped, her face growing redder with each passing second. With any luck, she'd match the color of my tank top.

"However, you can draw energy from people in other ways. The Academy advises us to ask permission and get their consent first, and don't get me started on the Sempiternal Code, but sometimes in a crowded room . . ." I shrugged, "we do what needs to be done."

"But in Silverwood Prison, they only gave us blood."

"We were also locked in a jail cell twenty-one hours a day with three hours in the yard in that blasted, abnormally bright sun."

She groaned. "Don't remind me. I don't want to relive that period ever again."

"And that's why you need to ask permission to draw energy when biting someone, because stale blood bags suck."

She extended her fangs and sucked in air through them, sounding like Hannibal Lecter á la *Silence of the Lambs*. "Suck. Get it?"

I raised an eyebrow. "Did you just make a joke?"

She smirked proudly. "I guess I did."

"Sisters and brothers, miracles happening right here."

"Speaking of brothers, will there be any tonight?"

"Looking for a quickie after our time in the clink?"

Her cheeks blazed again. She was so easy to mess with. Too easy, actually. I preferred more of a challenge.

"No . . . I just like . . . um, it's our Induction Ceremony into Silverwood Academy for those identifying as women."

"And . . ."

"After tonight, will we see any men during our time at the Academy?"

I sat down at the desk and pulled out a sketchbook and a pen. "Now, pay attention."

She leaned over my shoulder to watch. "I thought we were in a hurry."

"We've got time for this. We change once we get there anyway."

She stood up, putting her hands on her hips. "Seriously? I thought I had to wear this."

I grinned at her over my shoulder. "You had to wear something, and that other shirt made you look like a cloistered nun."

She sucked in a breath, her shoulders tensing. "It did not."

I turned back to the star I was drawing. "It did too, but lucky for you, I've got a wardrobe full of appropriate clothing."

"I bet."

I made a few more lines and circles. "Now, it's important to remember that for every nunnery, there's always a tunnel system to the priests' quarters."

"That's a myth."

"Not a myth. A legend based on fact. Luckily, Silverwood Academy is an equal opportunist." I made the finishing touches to the star, circle, and the five points and leaned back in my seat so Cyn could look.

She lifted the sketchbook and studied it. "What do all these lines mean?"

"Our building is shaped like a five-pointed star. Silverwood Prison circles around it, albeit in a different dimension, and beyond that circle is Wildwood Preserves. Each point of the star represents an element. One half represents the Divine Feminine along with the goddess that element represents. The second half represents the Divine Masculine along with the god that element represents."

Her forehead scrunched as she studied the map. "What if someone decides she or he stops identifying as she or he, or identifies as both, or doesn't identify as either?"

"Legitimate question, but you're thinking in terms of the gender roles that human society forces upon people. Our goddesses select based on the individual, as do the gods. They see and know all."

She backed away. "That doesn't sound creepy at all."

"It's the way of it. You'll get used to it and come to accept it, just like you've accepted me as your sister."

She set the drawing back on the desk. "I'm still pissed you turned me."

I rolled my eyes and stood up. "I didn't turn you. I merely sped up the process. Isn't it better to embrace who you are now than go through college and live a lie until the day you changed?"

"You keep saying that, but I don't believe you."

I swung open the door. "Well, believe it. Now, let's meet our goddess."

She scurried after me. I'd gotten into the habit of changing the subject or leaving anytime Cyn brought up how I forced her into this life. Which I totally did, but I also always told her the truth: The Change would have happened when she least expected it. Hell, it could have been on her wedding day. I had grown up with stories like the one about the wolf shifter who didn't emerge until she was exchanging vows with her partner. Rather than say "I do," she howled and fell to all fours. Her fiancé didn't take the Change too well and had stampeded over the fleeing guests—as a man, not as a fellow shifter. Luckily, Goddess Morrigan had sensed the Change coming and sent Guardians to assist the new wolf shifter and erase the memory of her change from all the attendees and her fiancé.

Typically supernaturals were descendants from past generations, but sometimes Mother Earth made surprise selections outside of her special children. Usually that was someone who demonstrated promise or who had caught her interest for some reason or another. Personally, I thought she liked to fuck with preconceived notions once in a while to keep everyone guessing. After all, she *was* the mother of freaking everyone. She could do whatever she wanted.

Of course, turned supernaturals also existed. Those who were bitten by a natural-born supernatural. Or rarer still, individuals who died when they had supernatural blood in their body. Both types took much longer to control their bloodlust and often found their fate entwined with a silver dagger or stake plunged through their heart. Of course, I kept the fate of turned supernaturals to myself rather than share it with Cynda. Sempiternal blood coursed through her veins. Destiny ensured she'd enter the Change. I just sped up the process.

I glanced over at her walking beside me. Today, we got along. Yesterday, not so much. Tomorrow, who knew what would happen? But I was glad we got to take the journey together. With Dad gone, and Mom most likely dead, Cyn was the only family I had left.

She pulled away from me. "Why are you looking at me like you want to cry?"

I reached my hand out to grab hers. "I'm just glad you're here."

She blew air out of her lips. "Whew. I thought you were going to tell me we were going to have to fight to our deaths or something like that tonight."

I winked at her. "Something like that."

She frowned. "Don't even start. I don't know you well enough to decipher when you're joking and when you're serious."

"I like keeping people on their toes."

"Lucky me," she mumbled.

A stream of other new initiates filtered out of their rooms, joining us on our walk to the ceremony. Male and female alike. The hallway grew with nervous excitement as more people joined us.

Soon our hallway joined with the other four points of the star, and everyone filtered into a pentagon-shaped courtyard. The ceremonies were held at the center of the star, but in separate locations by, you guessed it, magick.

"I thought we would have private spaces to change," Cyn whispered out of the corner of her mouth as she took in the wide-open area.

"The ceremony is sky-clad."

"What's that mean?"

"Nude. Naked. Tits, dicks, and butts exposed for all to see."

Her energy spiked with panic spilling off her into the air. I wrinkled my nose, my mouth turning down at the foulness. I hated the smell of worry and fear. It put a bad taste in my mouth. I didn't understand how some supes loved it, but then, they were usually the ones we hunted.

"We strip in front of everyone?"

I could keep messing with her, because it was fun, but her stress pheromones were making me sick.

"No."

The air instantly cleared, along with my desire to puke.

"Welcome," a feminine voice echoed through the air. "Daughters, please join me in your ceremonial clothing."

Cyn's head spun *Exorcist* style, searching for a private place to change, because she still wasn't entirely sure if we were supposed to get naked or not.

"Where do we get dressed?"

"Just keep walking."

Her head kept spinning, watching the rest of the initiates approach the center.

"Trust me."

"Not a fan of the lack of choices."

I sensed the energetic circle in front of us. I raised my hand to point toward it. "See?"

She squinted, her chin thrust forward as if it would help her see better. "See what?"

"The shimmering space right there."

"Right where?"

I rolled my eyes. Her lack of magickal experience annoyed me sometimes. A lot of times.

"Oh . . ." she sighed as we crossed over.

Tingles ran through my entire body as the tank top and jeans I wore transformed into a simple silver sheath dress.

"Wow." She played with the silky fabric of her own dress. "It's beautiful."

"It'll change color once our goddess selects us. Silver

represents Silverwood Academy, the united color of Silver Dagger Sisterhood and Silver Cloak Brotherhood."

As we entered the inner circle, a full moon hung overhead with thousands of stars flickering around it.

"Is this real or is it magick?"

"Can't they be the same thing?"

"I love magick." She sighed, staring up at the moon.

I smiled along with her. "Me too, Cyn. Me too."

CHAPTER
SIX

 yn

My FINGERS DANCED along the silky fabric, incapable of not playing with it. All the women smiled at their dresses, but none were as obsessed with touching the material as I was. Even Dez didn't seem compelled to feel the miraculous dress, simple in design yet somehow flattering to all figures.

I glanced around, realizing all the men had disappeared. I guess they really did have their own party to go to.

"Ladies, tonight is yours." A beautiful voice vibrated through and around us. "For this evening your goddess will select you, and each will host her own private Induction Ceremony. Which goddess will select you? Which element will rule you strongest? These are the same questions that every initiate has asked before they joined us, but know that each of my daughters, along with myself, Mother

Earth, will watch over you. Each element is available to you, but you must learn how to command each of them before you may wield them. Your body, mind, and spirit must work as one, and one day you may become members of Silver Dagger Sisterhood. The Sisters, along with Silver Cloak Brotherhood, watch over *all* my children, protecting them from those that stray, the evil forces who seek to destroy and control those perceived as weaker than them. While that could be your future, tonight is your present. Tonight is when you begin your journey to become Fairest Among The Absolute Lethal, a member of Silver Dagger Sisterhood."

"F.A.T.A.L.," Dez murmured beside me.

Mother Earth's voice was everywhere, echoing through our ears, our minds, our hearts, yet the only indication of a physical presence was a brilliant spectrum of light at the center of the circle. She was everywhere and nowhere.

Wow.

"I present to you initiates, my daughters who will guide you and preside over you during your time at Silverwood Academy and beyond. We are every race and no race."

Five beams of light shot down from the sky and landed at the different points of a five-pointed star that appeared before us. Lines crisscrossed, uniting them and joining them with Mother Earth's presence at the center. All things, all elements, revolved around her. I felt it in my bones, my blood, my soul.

"Rhiannon, Goddess of Sovereignty. Goddess of Horses. White Witch. Embodies Spirit."

A white-haired goddess appeared before us. A wreath of white flowers served as her crown. She wore a gorgeous white dress that hung past her knees, leaving only her bare feet exposed. Songbirds circled her head, but none sang a song. I could see her but couldn't make out her specific features. Her face was blurred by a blinding light shining down on her.

"Morrigan, Goddess of War. Goddess of Rivers and Lakes. Phantom Queen. Embodies Water."

A raven-haired goddess suddenly appeared. Black war paint masked her eyes. A large black bird, a raven I think, sat on her shoulder. Her red lips gave us a sideways grin as she took us all in, as if assessing our worth and perhaps even finding some of us lacking. She wore tight, dark blue leather that was almost black. She and my sister would get along well. She resonated with me, but it was probably because of her resemblance to Dez.

"Brigit, Goddess of Healers, Poets, and Childbirth. Goddess of Forge and Metalwork. Fiery Arrow. Embodies Fire."

Flames erupted from the third point of light. A red-haired goddess stepped out. She wore a red dress that looked as if it was made of fire. A small fire bloomed at my core.

"Maeve, Goddess of Love and Desire. Warrior Queen. Fairy Queen Mab. Embodies Earth."

Green vines shot from the ground at the fourth point of light. The vines twisted and spun into a beautiful goddess. Birds landed on her shoulders and arms. Small animals, including rabbits, squirrels, and chipmunks, scurried up her dress, taking their places up and along her arms and shoulders. But even with the adorable creatures sitting on her, she didn't give off a warm, fuzzy vibe. With her chest flared out and sharp eyes hinting at strong will and strength, a warrior vibe emanated from her.

"Finally, Lilith, Goddess of Night. Dark Champion of Women. Spirit of Great Ferocity. Embodies Air."

From the bright light of the fifth beam appeared a woman with yellow fabric draped across her important female parts but not much more. She left little to the imagination, and from the tilt of her head and her mischievous smirk, that was exactly how she liked it. Snakes curled around her arms, and a single owl was perched on her right shoulder. Something deep within me stirred awake at her presence. She called to me in a way that none of the other goddesses had. When she caught me gawking at her, she winked.

"She's Queen of the Vamps, Demons, and Witches too," Dez murmured beside me.

Yes, darkness wafted off her, but I wasn't afraid, and it wasn't because of the bright yellow drape she wore.

For the dark is only the opposite of light, a voice whispered in my head. I had the distinct feeling it was Lilith speaking directly to me.

"For some of you, one of my daughters calls to you in a way that the others do not."

Holy crap, did Mother Earth read my mind?

"I did not read your minds, dear children, for you are not the first to feel in such a way, nor will you be the last. All my special children require training to protect my innocent babes from those who have strayed." Mother Earth raised her arms and swung them out in front of her. "Each of these daughters represent Silver Dagger Sisterhood. My other children assist me with other matters, but these five and the elements they command will guide you through your time at Silverwood Academy and, if you succeed, into Silver Dagger Sisterhood."

I sensed rather than saw Mother Earth's gaze sweep over me, my sister, and the rest of the initiates.

"I call upon Water."

A small channel of water circled around Mother Earth and her daughters.

"I call upon Air."

A blast of air slammed into our faces, whooshing our breath away until filling our lungs with pure oxygen.

"What's happening?" I whispered to my sister.

"It's okay. Water and Air have revealed their presence."

"I call upon Fire."

Hot flames erupted in a circle around them.

"Glad my eyebrows didn't get scorched," Dez muttered out of the corner of her mouth. Her reaction made me laugh, immediately dispelling the growing unease in me. And dare I say, filling me with courage?

"I call upon Spirit."

Tingles ran up and down my spine, sending the hair on the back of my neck to stand on end. Goosebumps slid across my skin as a wavering presence circled the flames. Something that was there, but not quite.

"I call upon Earth."

The ground beneath our feet shook. A narrow crevice encircled the flames.

"Wow," Dez murmured. "That was intense."

I smiled to myself. At least I wasn't the only one freaked out and awed simultaneously.

"And we return to Water to complete the star. My children, each goddess is equally important, as is each element. I will circle around the points sun-wise or reversed, or I will follow the points of a star, changing the first each time. You will never know how I will share them with you, but know that none of my daughters or elements is more important than another. They all depend on each other to exist and coexist."

I agreed with Mother Earth. Each goddess and each

element gave off a potent level of energy with don't-fuck-with-me vibes.

"Your goal is to achieve balance with each of the elements. Unbalanced children are susceptible to Maleficium possession. You will learn how to fit into both worlds. The supernatural one and the earthly one."

Nothing Mother Earth said particularly alarmed me, but it could go south at any time.

"Now you wonder how your selection will take place."

Yes, actually I did, but if she didn't stop reading my head soon, I might actually lose my mind.

"You will walk through the circles in front of you. Through Spirit." The invisible wall wavered in front of us. "Do not underestimate that which you cannot see. It is always best to go through with your eyes wide open."

"Through Earth." The ground creaked and moaned as a subtle reminder that the narrow crack could widen at any time.

"Through Fire." Flames rose into the air, their challenge obvious.

"Through Air." A narrow windstorm erupted.

"And finally, through Water." The channel of water appeared the least difficult, but I suspected there was more to it than met the eye.

"You will reach into the Goddess Cauldron and withdraw a rune designating your goddess and your element. Hold the rune close to your heart. It will do the rest."

An enormous silver cauldron appeared next to Mother Earth. From my angle I could only make out two carved faces, Morrigan's and Lilith's. Both goddesses resonated with me in a way the others did not. I wasn't sure what that meant. I feared Lilith above all the goddesses. Her history was clouded in Christianity, and my parents—I glanced at

Dez—my *adoptive* parents were active in their church. I attended Sunday school, Bible study, the works. Lilith's Christianized story wasn't flattering, but she wouldn't have been part of this ceremony, Silverwood Academy, or Silver Dagger Sisterhood if she wasn't something amazing.

The runes intrigued me, just like every mention of magick always had. When I was little, I used to play with my next-door neighbor's daughter, Sophia. We threw her mom's runes for fun. We'd make predictions about the future. When my parents found out, I was banned from playing with Sophia or visiting her and her "witch mom." They used "witch" like it was a curse, but to me, the word had awakened something inside of me. Now I understood why.

Sophia's mom's runes seemed harmless enough, but I had a feeling these were far more powerful and potentially lethal.

"Anastasia, you may begin first," Mother Earth said.

A redhead stepped forward. She eyed the wavering wall in front of her and walked through it. It shimmered and sparkled as she passed through, but it didn't impede her. She made it to the other side and stood on the edge of the precipice. She glanced to her left, then to her right, as if checking for traffic before she leapt over it.

I caught Dez looking at me out of the corner of her eye. "That crevice must be much wider than it looks."

"Agreed."

The circle of flames shot up, creating a wall in front of Anastasia. Her chest rose and fell as she decided what she should do.

"Trust the process," Mother Earth whispered, her voice echoing through the chamber.

Anastasia bit her lip. She fingered her silky silver and highly flammable dress.

"Embrace your fire," a different voice whispered. Another fiery redhead stood at the flame symbol. Goddess Brigit.

Anastasia nodded, closed her eyes, and stepped through. Her dress didn't go up in flames. Her hair didn't light up on fire. Instead the flames embraced her as one of their own, kissing her cheeks, caressing her arms and legs. Anastasia smiled, hurried through Air and Water as if they were nothing at all, and plunged her hand into the Goddess Cauldron. Her hand felt around inside. Her eyes lit up in excitement when she found her rune. She withdrew it and clutched it in her left hand. Suddenly, her silver dress changed to red. Her eyes widened in shock as she dropped the rune into her right hand and waved her left palm. There was Fire emblem emblazoned on it.

"They mark us like cattle," I whispered.

"Not like cattle; like future members of the Sisterhood," Dez replied.

I huffed a breath. I wasn't sure how I felt about that.

"Deziree, you are next," Mother Earth said.

Guess, we'd find out soon enough.

SEVEN

ez

"Deziree, you are next." Mother Earth's voice vibrated around me and through me.

I tried to keep a nonchalant expression on my face, but my insides were like, *Holy mother fucker, it's time.*

Dad had told me all about his induction into Silverwood Academy and ultimately his entrance into Silver Cloak Brotherhood, but he could only speak from the male experience. The masculine approach to the elements involved blades, bloodshed, and testosterone. Anastasia's experience didn't resemble any of the stories he'd shared with me, and since my mother had disappeared at Cyn's birth, I had only my wits, a brazen attitude, and my training to help me.

I took a deep breath in and out and stepped forward. The air around Spirit's circle crackled with electricity. Anastasia hadn't gotten zapped or anything, but maybe her internal fire had quelled it. I ground my bare feet into the stone floor, wishing I still wore my Docs. Their rubber soles would ground me from the initial shocks and any after-shocks that might occur. I pulled at the silk dress. Nothing in the fabric to protect me.

"Whenever you are ready, you may proceed," Mother Earth reminded me, in case I'd forgotten.

Here goes nothing.

I stepped through the wavering circle, jerking and twisting as thousands of tiny bolts of electricity shot through me.

"Holy Mother!" I blurted once I made it to the other side.

"Holy Mother doesn't reside here. Only I do."

Great. Mother Earth had a snarky personality too.

I now stood on the edge of an enormous cliff. No wonder Anastasia had hesitated. From the other initiates' perspective, Earth's circle was a tiny crevice, but now, standing over it, it was a gaping chasm. I leaned over and looked down—with apparently no bottom.

Anastasia had jumped it. I eyed the distance. I was tall, my legs were long and powerful, and my arms were strong. Even if I shorted it, I could pull myself up on the other side. Only problem was heights freaked me out. I preferred ground level.

Trust in yourself, a voice whispered in my head. I glanced up and looked at Maeve. She winked as she smiled at me.

I shifted my legs into a lunge, rocking toe to heel, toe to heel.

I can do this. I can do this, I chanted to myself.

Yes, you can.

For a few months, Dad and I had lived in a small town while

he hunted a rogue shifter posing as a demon posing as a custodian in the school—huge Freddy Krueger fan who took his obsession too far. He even lived on Elm Street—dead giveaway. While there, I had joined the track team in an effort to test my growing athletic prowess and to make friends. (I was stupidly optimistic then.) Sprinting, distance running, jumping—I loved all of it and burned my coach's suggestions to memory.

I narrowed my eyes at the opening and pushed off the stone floor as if long-jumping. I flew across and landed on the other side with both feet together, just like my coach had taught me. I pitched my body forward onto my hands and knees so I wouldn't fall back in the sand—or in this case, fall off the cliff.

But before I could get too excited about my success, a circle of flames shot up in front of me, threatening to singe my dress. I jumped up and brushed my hands off, staring at the flames dancing in front of me. Fire always mesmerized me. Fire, in all its forms, whether a spell candle, a bonfire, a torch, or even a single match, deserved respect. A small flame could cause incredible damage.

Again I eyed the silk dress. Based on Anastasia's experience, it was flame retardant, at least it had been for her, but the question was, would it protect me? And would it turn to red like hers did once I completed the challenges? Or would I complete them and not find my element? I'd never admit it to anyone, but I had never felt like any element called to me louder than another. In truth, I feared them all.

Fear can be manipulated. Fear throws a person off-balance. Lessons of my father came back to me, but in this moment, none of that mattered.

The fire before me heated my skin, burned my cheeks, threatened to cook me to a crisp.

Child, do not fear me or my fire, for I have much to teach you. I would choose you, but you are already spoken for.

I stilled as I stared at the flames. Someone already spoke for me?

Of course. Your gifts are many. Each of my sisters recognizes the service you will provide all our children. We look forward to training you, but one desires you above all.

I looked over at Brigit, unable to believe it was really her speaking in my head and that what she was telling me was true. I was desirable?

She threw back her head and laughed for all the initiates to witness. "Yes. Now, go."

My conversation with Brigit gave me courage. All the goddesses wanted me, but one wanted me more than the others. I studied the fire. The flames formed a wall too high to jump, even if I had a pole to pole-vault with. I remembered the fire walkers Dad and I had met during one of his missions. They claimed mind over matter worked. I put the heat and the height of the flames out of my mind and walked through them. Flames kissed my cheeks, cradled my arms, and embraced my body but didn't burn me or stop me from passing through. When I got to the other side, I sighed in relief. Three down. Only Lilith and Morrigan remained. One of whom wanted me. Both badass goddesses often scorned because they were the most misunderstood of the five goddesses.

I'd be happy with either of them. Hells, I would have been happy with Rhiannon, Maeve, or Brigit. Each goddess could teach me things.

A windstorm picked up in front of me. Objects shot around in the air. I peeked closer. Were those daggers?

Does that scare you? Are you afraid? Lilith taunted. There wasn't anything kind or encouraging about her voice compared to the other goddesses'.

If you seek sympathy, you've come to the wrong goddess.

So that was how it was going to be? I grinned to myself. Being raised by a member of Silver Cloak Brotherhood hadn't included coddling or touchy-feelies. Sure, he could clean and stitch a knife wound better than any doctor, even though his methods did not include numbing ointments. And rather than teddy bears and stuffed unicorns, I had learned how to fight real bear shifters and actual unicorns, which might fart glitter rainbows, but their horn could kill you. So, yes, I could handle Lilith and all her bitchiness.

I reached both hands into the windstorm and snagged two daggers. I swung them back and forth, testing their weight and their potential killing ability. When I was satisfied that they were in fact real, sharp, and deadly, I jabbed them into the windstorm and stepped through. I ducked, twirled, and swung my way through the blades, receiving only a single scratch across my bicep.

A bright yellow light shot down, and my dress changed to yellow. I glared at Lilith and shot her the finger. Her eyes sparkled with mischief as she returned it.

"Welcome, Dark Champion of Women, future protector of the innocent, Daughter of Night."

I bowed and strode through the channel of Water as if it were nothing at all. I plunged my hand into the Goddess Cauldron and withdrew a rune with the elemental sign of Air on it. I cried out as a sharp blade dug into my left palm. When I opened it, I saw the mark of Air, the mark of Lilith there.

A single tear ran down my cheek. Lilith chose me. She claimed me.

Please choose Cynda too.

Her eyes met mine. *Another wants her.*

More tears escaped from my eyes. I swiped them away. Tears were weak. Sympathy wouldn't work on Lilith.

I need her. She's family.

She raised her chin. *All the children of my House are your family.*

Cynda is blood.

I will see how she does in the challenges. If she can champion the windstorm, I will allow her entrance.

"Cynda, it is your turn," Mother Earth said.

Cyn's face paled. Her eyes met mine. "I can't do this," she mouthed.

I glared at her. "Yes, you can. Now, go."

She stepped into the wavering Spirit circle and got knocked backward on her ass.

Shit, maybe she couldn't do this.

CHAPTER
EIGHT

yn

MY SISTER HAD WORKED the Elemental Challenges like a badass ninja warrior. The way she jabbed those daggers through the windstorm? Holy crow! I didn't even know where she had gotten them. It looked like she'd pulled them out of thin air. Geez, maybe she had.

"Cynda, it is your turn," Mother Earth said.

All the color ran out of my face. My palms got sweaty. My forehead broke out in a cold sweat. I wasn't ready. I wasn't a warrior. I barely had control over my bloodlust. I was soft. Nonathletic. A bookworm. I hadn't been raised with daggers and swords, or with supernaturals, or with my dad.

"I can't do this."

Dez narrowed her eyes at me. "Yes, you can. Now, go."

The force of her words propelled me forward into the

flickering Spirit circle. But I wasn't ready. I needed time to think.

To contemplate.

To— I flung my body backward to avoid the surge of electricity pulsing through the wall.

—To land on my ass.

I winced. Ouch, that hurt.

I pushed myself back up. The lessons I had learned in Silverwood Prison were clear. Don't get control of your bloodlust? Die. Leap into the abnormally bright sun without taking magickal precautions? Die. Leap into a fight of angry shifters? You guessed it, also die. And I would have if Dez hadn't yanked me out and kicked shifter ass all over the prison yard.

I eyed the wall of energy. Power surged through it like an electric horse fence. It wasn't constant. I breathed in and out, waiting to strike. Right after the surge shot through, I dove into the wall and face-planted on the other side. Dez had landed far more gracefully, but I'd made it through, and that was all that mattered.

One down, four to go.

I eyed the crevice. The Grand Canyon would be less traumatic, because at least I could hike down the trail and walk up the other side. Sure, it might take a while, but like the tortoise, slow and steady won the race.

I paced along the edge of it. Heights didn't bother me. I'd spent my childhood climbing trees. That's why I had tried to escape Silverwood Prison by climbing the fence— which was an epic fail. I didn't anticipate the raging lava pit on the other side of it. The guards let me hang there for three hours as punishment before retrieving me.

A downed tree would be nice.

Just as the thought left my mind and entered the

universe, a giant tree appeared, stretching from one side of the chasm to the other. Without hesitating, I scurried across it.

"Not so bad, if I do say so myself."

I agree with you. Well done, a voice echoed through my head, but it wasn't Mother Earth.

Maeve?

At your service. I look forward to working with you and your sister, but for now, you must continue.

Fire erupted in front of me.

I had loved camping with my family and eating s'mores when I was little. There wasn't anything better than a campfire. My mom, well evidently my adoptive mom, drilled into me to respect fire in all its forms, including the ashes left in the firepit the next day, because beneath the ashy debris resided hot coals that could be brought back to life. All they needed was a gust of oxygen and . . . towering inferno. But a healthy dose of water would put out the flames and the coals for good.

A bucket of water appeared in front of me.

I looked around, wondering if someone was reading my mind or at least supplying me with the things I needed to succeed this challenge. There was no way I was manifesting this stuff.

Never underestimate your abilities. You have many.

The voice didn't belong to Maeve or Mother Earth. *Brigit?*

Yes, child. Both you and your sister are so surprised that we speak to you during the challenges. As Mother Earth suggested, we do not abandon our children. We may not always be available to help, but we're always present. Hold on to that. Now, it is time for you to move forward.

I picked up the bucket, threw it over the flames, and

jumped across. I landed with enough grace to congratulate myself. I would have given myself a pat on the back if no one was watching.

The windstorm picked up in front of me. I peered through, remembering the lake from my hometown. Strong winds had enabled me to fly across the water on my wind-surfer. I wasn't afraid of its presence, but like fire, I respected it. A sudden gust could have caused me to fly into freezing water if I wasn't paying attention, or it could die down, leaving me stranded in the middle of the lake. And when the winds were too strong, it was easy to be carried far down the lake, but it was a battle, taking skill and finesse, to get back to shore. A few of the other girls at the lake had enjoyed playing the damsel in distress, waiting for the safety boat to come to their rescue, but that had never sat well with me. Whenever it was too windy or not windy enough, I went ahead and sailed or paddled back by myself. My mom would always quote Frances Hodgson Burnett. "She made herself stronger by fighting with the wind."

I was strong. I did not fear it. I stepped into it. The wind kissed my cheeks. It cradled my arms and lifted me up, twirling me around the circle once, before dropping me on the other side.

My child, you surprised me, and I am not surprised easily.

Lilith?

Yes, and if you agree, it will honor me for you to join my Daughters of Night, Dark Champions of Women.

One time at the lake, two of my friends who had always waited for someone to rescue them were invited to a party by two of their "saviors." That night, the bastards raped them. I couldn't help my friends, but if I could prevent other women from predators of all forms, I would do it.

Yes.

Lilith grinned at me and snapped her fingers. My dress changed to yellow.

I spun around to look at Dez. Her face beamed at me when she realized I was wearing yellow. I smiled back. For once in my life, I truly felt I was where I was supposed to be.

I leapt over Water and dipped my hand into the Goddess Cauldron. Several runes jumped at me, as if wanting me to select them, but there was one element that called to me more than the others. One whose color I already bore. My fingers wrapped around the rune, and I pulled it to my chest. A warm breeze kissed my cheeks as I felt a gentle sting in my palm. When it was over, I placed the rune in my other hand and studied Air's symbol. I glanced up one more time and met Dez's purple eyes. She frowned when I held up my palm for her. She had cried out when she received hers. She also bore a gash on her arm from her time in the windstorm. It was clear our challenges were different, but I didn't understand why. It didn't seem fair.

Everyone completes the Elemental Challenges in their own way. Each goddess tests differently, depending on what they are searching for as well as the initiate's strengths and weaknesses. You performed well, and your actions were rewarded.

I raised my chin, my chest flaring out. I had never felt so proud in my entire life. I returned to Dez's side and watched the remainder of the initiates pass through the Elemental Challenges. Each one entered and left the elemental circle in a different manner, but every one of them had entered with a silver silk dress and, by the end of it, left with the color embodying their goddess and element.

"Children," Mother Earth said finally, when the last of the initiates had completed the challenges, "each goddess requests that you meet her to complete your induction into

Silverwood Academy. You will receive your new room assignments based on your element."

Rumbles rushed through the crowd, everyone worrying about their belongings.

Mother Earth raised her hand, and the initiates immediately fell silent. "Not to worry, your personal effects will be set up in your new rooms. Your wardrobe for Silverwood Academy will also be hung in your closets and put away in your dressers. During your classes, you will wear your elemental colors and symbols. Wear them with pride, for it means you were selected, just as you were selected to come here. Most supernaturals do not receive such an invitation. Use your time here wisely, for only the most talented, the most skilled, will be asked to join Silver Dagger Sisterhood."

I stilled. We had to be invited to join Silver Dagger Sisterhood? I had thought graduates would automatically be inducted into it.

Dez tapped my shoulder. "You all right? You look dazed and confused, but not in a good way."

"You said we would enter Silver Dagger Sisterhood after the Academy. You never mentioned we had to get invited."

Her forehead bunched. "Figured you knew that."

I rolled my eyes, clenching my fists. The excitement of my completion of the challenges and my invite from Lilith was gone. My patience with my sister wore thin. Again. "How would I know that? I didn't even know supernaturals existed, let alone that there were academies and sisterhoods. I question if I'll be able to get through the Academy, let alone pass some kind of test for the Sisterhood."

She waved her hand in the air like I was some kind of pesky fly. "You killed it during the Elemental Challenges. Silverwood Academy will be a no-brainer."

"You say that now, but . . ."

A blinding presence appeared in front of us, dressed in her barely there yellow drape. "Ladies, is there a problem?"

Dez cracked her neck. "No problem. First day jitters is all."

"Humph," Lilith said, which didn't sound goddess-like in the least.

She grabbed our hands. An invisible force pushed us toward her. "You both shine brightly in yellow. Please, follow me."

"Don't worry about Silver Dagger Sisterhood. You're a natural," Dez whispered out of the corner of her mouth.

"Said every liar ever," I hissed.

NINE

D^{ez}

EVERY TIME I even thought about lifting my head, my stomach rolled over. In my mind, the room was spinning like a freaking Tilt-a-Whirl. Lilith knew how to throw a party, and my, how I'd partied. Cyn had loosened up as the evening wore on, but she continued to act like I'd betrayed her for some reason. Not that I wasn't used to it by now, but still, I don't know why she was so freaked out about needing an invitation to join Silver Dagger Sisterhood. She was a shoo-in and so was I. I mean, not many could say their mother was a member of the Sisterhood or that their dad was a member of Silver Cloak Brotherhood, or that they were destined to hunt rogue supernaturals and slay those who refused to comply. And we were Sempiternals—that gave us automatic street cred.

"Would you get your ass up?" Cyn growled for the fifth time. "I don't want to be late."

I groaned, clutching my head. Great. My little sister was one of those . . . If only she were a witch and could whip up some hangover potion. I gotta get me one of those.

"Know any witches?"

"No, I only know you."

"My head's killing me."

"Not my fault you drank so much. What did you expect would happen?"

Great, she was an I-told-you-so person too. I hated that kind, especially with a hangover. I hated most kinds, actually, which was why I thought maybe my sister would make an adequate companion to me during our time at Silverwood Academy and beyond. I stood corrected.

"Get up. I already laid out your outfit for you."

I sat up, frowning at the pile of clothes on my bed. "You picked clothes out for me?"

She adjusted the collar of her yellow blouse. "I didn't pick them out. They're our school uniform. Remember?"

I climbed out of bed, and our new room started spinning again. I curled into a ball on the floor. "Awww," I whimpered.

She snapped her fingers in front of my face.

I jerked my head up. "Is that supposed to help?"

"No, not at all. It's to get you moving."

I rolled onto my stomach and rested my head against my hands. "Imma just gonna sleep a little longer."

She clucked her tongue. "Suit yourself. Your schedule's on the desk. I'll see you later."

She swung open the door. Freezing air whooshed into the room, wrapped around my body, and placed me into a standing position.

"What the hell?"

Lilith appeared in the doorway, wearing a smart yellow pantsuit. Her short hair was styled carefully up and away from her face, and her high heels gave me a nosebleed just looking at them. She took off her dark sunglasses and flung them over. "Here. You need these more than I do."

I caught them and put them on, instantly feeling better. I pulled them down my nose and the world went sideways again. I pushed them back on. "They're magicked?"

She winked at me as she stepped out of the room. "Stick with me kid. You'll pick up a thing or two or ten."

"I guess so." I yanked off my crumpled yellow sheath dress and pulled on black leather pants and a black tank top with a yellow Air symbol embroidered on it. I glanced over at Cyn who also wore black leather pants, but she had a fitted yellow blouse with a black embroidered Air symbol.

"This is my uniform?"

"Guess so."

I liked that we didn't have to dress exactly the same. Tank tops were more me than blouses.

"Don't forget your boots."

I slid into new black Docs with bright yellow stitching. Once I laced them, I strode over to the door. I could get behind this uniform.

Cyn raised an eyebrow at me. "Aren't you forgetting something?"

I patted my body as if there was something on me. "What?"

She pointed at my hair. "Don't you want to brush it?"

I ran my fingers through my hair, smoothing down errant strands as I went. "I'm good."

She pursed her lips, patting her perfectly curled locks. "If you say so."

"I do. I definitely do. Now, let's eat."

"Don't forget your schedule. Grab your books too."

I rushed over to my desk. "We already got our books?" I gave the spines a quick once-over. *Herbology*, *History of Weaponry*, *Spiritual Alchemy*, *Elemental History* . . . I freaking loved Silverwood Academy.

I perused my schedule as I walked back to her. "What the . . . I've got Meditation and Yoga first thing? What the fuck good will that do? Can I slay an evil faerie with a sun salutation? I don't think so."

Lilith pursed her lips but remained quiet out in the hall.

"Guess, you'll have to tell me after my Weapons Training class."

I snatched my sister's schedule off the top of her books. "We don't have the same schedule? That's crap."

The tendon in her jaw hinted she agreed with me, but she wasn't about to admit that to anyone, let alone her sister.

"We have Riding together tomorrow morning."

"I hope it's not with horses. Horses and I don't mesh." I'd never get that stampeding, fire-breathing, morphed herd of unicorns out of my mind for as long as I lived.

"Oh, I don't know. You both make loud chewing noises when you eat. And I always have to sidestep your shit."

I glared at her. "Not funny."

She laughed. "It's kinda funny."

"Why did I change you again?"

She sobered up quickly. "You didn't want to be alone."

Sometimes I hated that I was such a bitch, but only sometimes. "Right, that."

Lilith popped her head back into the room. "Ladies, we'll eat breakfast together today, but after that you're free to comingle with the others as you see fit. As new initiates, you may be tempted to stick with members of the same House, but Silverwood Academy doesn't want you to blindly follow rules or conform to the status quo."

"Says the goddess who requires us to wear clothing with a symbol embroidered on it rather than our own digs."

Her gaze pinned me in place. "Tell me, Dez, you wouldn't select black leather pants and a black tank top? You don't want to wear black combat boots? Fine." She snapped her fingers, and suddenly I was wearing a yellow ball gown with heels, and the magickal hangover-curing sunglasses were gone. My temples pounded against my brain from the headache *and* elevation sickness.

She crossed her arms, daring me to argue with her. "How do you feel about *this* uniform?"

I was many things, but a liar wasn't one of them. "You're right. I would select black leather pants and black tank tops if given the choice."

"And the Docs?"

"I will always wear Docs. Always."

She smirked, snapping her fingers. "Very well then."

A wave of energy pulsed through me. I glanced down to find myself in my standard-issue clothing.

"Your clothes were selected based on your tastes."

I followed her and Cyn into the hall, joining the other initiates. Indeed, everyone wore vastly different clothing. The only similarities were the touches of yellow and the Air symbol embroidery. Even our footwear was different.

I frowned at Cyn's black leather pants. "You chose them?" They didn't remotely resemble anything I'd ever seen her wear during the time I'd observed her, pre-vampire. Like any good hunter, I had spent a few days watching her to get an idea of her routine, her lifestyle. And to assess if she really was my sister.

Her cheeks blushed. "I was given black leggings, but then I touched yours when I set them out for you and they were so soft and supple, so I tried them on and never took them off."

I raised an eyebrow. "So those are mine too."

She blushed but lifted her chin in a subtle act of defiance or courage—take your pick. "Yes."

"Smart choice. Dirt, blood, and other stains don't show up on black leather. Though I can't say the same for that yellow shirt."

She adjusted the collar again. "Oh, I didn't think of that."

Lilith materialized between us. "Want me to change it?"

Cyn's eyes met mine, and she nodded.

Lilith snapped her fingers and Cyn's shirt changed to black. Lilith also changed into a similar outfit, even down to scuffed Docs. She spun back around and veered toward the yellow tables in the open-air courtyard.

I bit my lip, watching the Goddess of Night. Queen of Vampires. Dark Protector of the Innocent. I glanced over at Cyn who was also watching Lilith. All the color drained from her face. I hoped she could handle the goddess, since I had made the choice for her. Again.

False. I wanted her from the beginning as I wanted you, though I did not disclose that to you. Your sister wanted to stay close to you. The specific goddess didn't matter to her.

I straightened, surprised at Lilith's disclosure. My sister chose me. *Me.* My eyes watered. Warmth spread from my heart up to my head and down to my toes. This was what love felt like . . .

Wow.

"What?" Cyn asked in concern.

"Nothing. Let's go eat."

CHAPTER
TEN

yn

IN FRONT OF DEZ, I acted confident, as if this new life didn't completely freak me out, but the truth was I was terrified. Silverwood Academy and all the classes pushed me a million miles outside my comfort zone. I mean before Dez kidnapped and killed me, I had been about to leave for college on a STEM scholarship. Science, Technology, Engineering, and Math were a far cry from Weapons Training, Herbology, Ghostbusting, and Spiritual Alchemy—although that last one might somehow connect to my prior life path. I knew nothing about weapons or how to use them. At least I got Yoga and Meditation. I loved meditating, and yoga was my kind of physical exertion. I didn't like sweat, though. I stayed away from hot yoga for a reason, and I didn't want to break that trend now, but here I was, heading to a class in the dungeon—a freaking dungeon. Nothing like perpetuating a stereotype of scary-ass shit. I pushed through the bulky carved wood doors and entered an enormous green space filled with trees, draping vines, grass, and . . . sunlight? I backed out and double-checked my surroundings. Torches lit the hallway I had come down.

A cluster of students appeared at the foot of the stairs and were coming my way.

"Is this Weapons Training?" a red-haired girl asked. I recognized her from last night.

"Anastasia, right?"

Her green eyes lit up with excitement. "You were kick-ass with your handling of Earth. Great use of the resources around you."

"Thanks. You were incredible with Spirit. That electricity was tricky."

"Thanks." She offered me her hand. "Anastasia, as you already know, and you're . . ." her eyes blurred as she concentrated, probably trying to recall my name from the Induction Ceremony. "Cynda. You're Cynda."

"I am. Nice to meet you."

"You as well."

A girl standing next to Anastasia cleared her throat.

"Oh, sorry," Anastasia said. "Azalea, meet Cynda. Cynda, Azalea."

I offered my hand to her, but she refused to shake it.

Anastasia glanced down at her. "Azalea's still working on controlling her abilities. Unless you want a rosebush growing out of your hand, I'd skip the handshake."

Definitely not what I expected, but okay.

"Right. Nice to meet you, Azalea."

"And you."

I took in her petite frame, silvery-purple hair, and pale

skin. None of the supernaturals in Silverwood Prison lined up with her characteristics. "What are you?"

Azalea's face darkened. "That's not something you ask."

I raised my hands, realizing my mistake. "Sorry. I'm new to this world. I didn't even know supernaturals actually existed until a few weeks ago."

She crossed her arms, and violets popped up across them. She growled as she wiped them off and skirted around me to enter the classroom.

"I really didn't mean to offend her."

Anastasia waved off my concern. "Not a big deal. Some are more sensitive than others." She leaned in and whispered. "Especially pixies."

"Pixies?" I mouthed.

She nodded, her lip curling into a grin.

"Wow."

"I'm a witch, in case you were wondering."

"Cool. Witches are real too? More than just dedicated pagans?"

She lifted her left hand and a red flame rose from it. "Dedicated pagan witches to be exact. Some more powerful than others."

"I'm a vampire. A Sempiternal."

She winked. "I could tell."

I stiffened. The black shirt and black leather should hide any blood I might have dripped on myself at breakfast, and I only drank three mouthfuls. Granted they were large mouthfuls, but still.

"Don't worry. There's no blood dripping down your chin. I just know things. I saw us become friends."

"So you're a seer. Is that what it's called?"

She moved to my ear. "Keep that between us for now. I only told you because I know I can trust you."

63

I nodded, my excitement positively swelling. But I tried to play it cool. "Right, right. You can totally trust me."

She laughed as she looped her arm through mine, and we walked into the wide-open space together.

Azalea's eyes narrowed in on our hooked arms. She pursed her lips, glaring at me.

I swallowed. Anastasia felt like an instant bestie. She was all warm and fuzzy without any regard for someone else's personal space. Azalea, contrary to her name, wasn't very welcoming, and the vibes she gave off said, "Leave me alone." And I intended to.

"I love magick," Anastasia sighed as we entered the strange outdoor space together.

I spun around with her still holding on to me as I took it all in. "We *are* in the dungeons, right?"

She covered her mouth, trying not to laugh. "You really are new, aren't you?"

"I am, but I'm practical. We walked down several flights of stairs to get here."

"You were in Silverwood Prison, right?"

"Unfortunately, yes. For far longer than I wanted."

"No one wants to go to Silverwood Prison. We were all stuck there for way too long."

Of course, I understood why Dez and I had been there. As newly turned vamps, we needed to get control over our bloodlust. But what would a witch have to control? Or other supernaturals, for that matter? I planned to ask Anastasia sometime but didn't want to push the boundaries of our newly forged friendship.

"Did you wonder why we were bombarded by constant sunlight, even when Northeast Pennsylvania is known for cloudy skies and long, dark months of winter?" she asked.

"I wasn't in the right frame of mind to question the

hows and the whats or the whys, but now that you mention it, it was strange. That and I didn't even know we were in Pennsylvania."

"Welcome to P.A.," she grinned, patting my back. "But you have noticed that there hasn't been a mention of Silverwood Prison since our entrance into Silverwood Academy, yet it encircles it?"

She did make a point, but she kept forgetting one vital aspect. "You forget, I didn't grow up with supernaturals."

"Oh yeah." She snapped her fingers. Wisps of green smoke circled out of them. She spread her palm out wide and a map appeared. On it was a building shaped like a pentagram with two circles around it. Two more enormous circles encircled the entire location. I peered closer. The outer circles were labeled Silverwood Prison. I looked at her. Her magickal 3-D map resembled Dez's drawing, but it didn't explain the mystery of our outdoor dungeon classroom or the prison.

"Still don't understand."

"Entrance and exit to Silverwood Prison is via portal. The prison is in an alternate dimension. A prison dimension, if you will."

A lightbulb went off in my head. Dez had mentioned the prison was in another dimension, but I hadn't really known what she meant. "So you're saying that even though we walked down to the dungeon, we're not actually in the dungeons."

She threw her hands up and fanned them out. "She can be taught, ladies and gentlemen."

Dozens of eyes landed on me. Fantastic. I wanted to snap my fingers and disappear. I hated being the center of attention, but clearly she didn't have a problem with it.

She wrapped her arm around mine again and pulled me

into the open space. "Sorry everyone looked at you. Sometimes I get carried away."

"You don't say, Red."

She giggled. "I couldn't wait for you to call me that. The instant I heard it in my dream, I loved it."

I squinted at her, my own red curls coming into my sight. "You've never been called Red before? Seriously? Did you live under a rock prior to coming here?"

The sparkle in her eyes dimmed. "Something like that."

I immediately regretted teasing her. Dez rubbed off on me. I patted her arm. It was my turn to make her feel better. "We're here now."

Her fire relit. "Yes, we are, bestie."

Bestie. I liked the sound of that. I had never actually had a bestie growing up. I never fit in as well as everyone else seemed to, and once Dez turned me, friendship seemed out of the realm of possibility. Glad I was wrong.

A tall, thin woman walked into the center of the green space. "Welcome to Weapons Training. We'll begin with swordplay. Go grab one."

A sword rack appeared next to her, and she walked away from it.

Murmurs of discontent whirled up around me, combined with awkward shuffling and the stink of uncertainty.

"She can't be serious."

"Battle with a sword? Is she crazy?"

Glad I wasn't the only one hesitant about touching them, let alone fighting with one. I had cut my finger slicing a bagel the day I left for college. Sharp blades and Cynda didn't get along well. Oh Goddess, I sounded just like my sister with horses. She really was rubbing off on me. I still couldn't decide if that was good or bad. Probably both.

The instructor put her hands on her hips, and everyone went silent. Not a word was murmured. Not a finger wiggled. Not an eyebrow twitched. Her presence alone was enough to shut people up.

"You are wise not to handle a weapon until you are familiar with it. However," she raised a single finger, "you must not, I repeat, must not, *ever* let your opponent observe your hesitation. As far as he, she, or they know, you are as trained in swordplay as anyone who has ever lived. Well, other than me." She winked, and the tension immediately dissipated. "Your singular goal is to enter Silver Dagger Sisterhood or Silver Cloak Brotherhood. That's why you're here. That's why you were chosen to attend this academy." Her silvery-blue eyes studied each person present. "You were all chosen."

My ears tingled as she spoke. I wondered if it was magick or if she struck a chord with everyone as much as she did with me. Dez kept insisting I would have changed regardless of her actions. Of course, I wanted to deny that fact, but I couldn't deny the way I felt last night or now.

"I am Lara Bladecroft."

She had to be joking. Way too close to the *Tomb Raider* main character. And instructor of Weapons Training? I mean, come on.

"You might think I jest or that my parents ripped off the popular movie and game." Her arms shot across her chest, and she whipped out two blades faster than a viper strike. She crouched into a low lunge. Her hair was tied back in a braid, and her pointed ears were prominently displayed. Every muscle in her body coiled to strike. "I assure you that two hundred years ago, that fictional character did not exist. However, I did."

She swung her arms around as she twirled in the air,

her legs kicking out, her long braid whipping around, and her blades narrowly missing several classmates, including Azalea, whose face paled as she clutched her stomach, blinking hard.

Anastasia gasped. "You're the elf warrior who Lara Croft is based on. I always wondered if the rumors were true."

Lara Bladecroft relaxed her stance and returned her blades to their sheaths. "Indeed. Now, who's ready for some sword instruction?"

Every hand shot up, including my own.

Lara Bladecroft had won us over, sword, blade, and kick-ass heroine.

CHAPTER
ELEVEN

D^{ez}

CONTRARY TO POPULAR belief and what I fed my sister, vampires didn't subsist on blood alone. We enjoyed most human food, especially pizza, but my breakfast along with the tequila from the night before wasn't sitting so well in my stomach.

I wasn't crazy about taking a Meditation and Yoga class, period, let alone as my first class at the Academy, but when the hunky piece of manflesh came in and instructed us to lie down and get comfortable, I followed his directions without argument, even removing Lilith's sunglasses when he requested me to. There would be plenty of time for role-play conversations later. Now was the time to kick this hangover to the curb and maybe take a nap. Although I did regret not brushing my hair before class, or my teeth.

Of course, I knew the Academy served women and men.

My brain was just too thick to latch on to the notion that the opposite sex would be lying on yoga mats all around me and that the instructor probably knew a thing or two about kundalini sex—and I wanted a private tutoring session.

Just thinking about what that experience might include tightened everything below my belly button in the best of ways.

"You okay over there, vamp?" whispered the guy next to me.

Damn shifters and their sensitive noses.

"Yeah, I'm fine."

"If you've got an itch after class, I'll scratch it for you."

"Is that before or after I run a dagger through your throat?"

He chuckled. "So that's how it's going to be between us?"

"That's how it is, and there is no 'between us.'"

Soft footsteps padded over and stopped at the end of the mat above my head. If I looked up, I'd get an eyeful of everything that made him a man, and if my presence excited him, I would know.

"Everything all right over here?"

"Just peachy. I established some boundaries with my neighbor. Now he's aware I don't play nice."

Hunky cleared his throat. "We're not playing right now. We're practicing meditation."

"Yep. Gotcha. No more side conversations here."

"Silent meditation."

"Got it. Meditating away."

"We'll see," he said with a touch of smugness and definitely a hint of snide. As Queen of Sarcasm, it took everything in me not to answer back, but I really was trying. The faster I got through the Academy, the faster I got into Silver

Dagger Sisterhood, the faster I could find my father's killer and return the favor.

I closed my eyes and tried to "still my mind" as Hunky suggested. Trouble was, my mind raced around like a squirrel searching for nuts. Oh wait, squirrel! Oh snap, nut! Oh yes, acorn!

See what I mean?

And my head pounded like a holy mother fanger. Breakfast, the smoothie, the coffee, the orange juice—nothing cut the ache in my temples. That was the last time I would ever challenge a goddess to shots. Freaking Lilith was a drinking beast.

I threw up my hands and slammed them against the mat. "It's no use. I can't do it."

Footsteps hurried over, and Hunky squatted beside me. "Can't do what?" His deep, low voice didn't help matters.

"Why do I need to take a class on meditation anyway? How is this," I circled my hands in the air, "going to help me fight evil?"

"Can't or won't?"

"Excuse me. We're past that. Now, I'm asking why I need to meditate."

"Can't or won't?" he pressed.

"Ugh, does it matter?"

"In the long term, yes. In the short term, try a pagan prayer bead."

I sat up. Hunky was persistent, I'd give him that, but he'd chosen the wrong person to mess with this morning. Time for me to go.

As if sensing my intentions, he shoved a white, almost-translucent bowl in front of me. I had no choice but to look at the contents. Indeed a bunch of beads, charms, and tassels were clustered inside it.

I caressed the smooth sides of the bowl. Warmth exuded from it. "What's the bowl made out of?"

He folded his legs into a seated position. "Interesting that you ask about the composite of the bowl rather than jump to most people's first question, which is, are they rosary beads?"

I twirled my hands in the air. "You called them pagan prayer beads, so obviously they're different from rosary beads, which are connected primarily to Catholicism. The word 'pagan' makes it crystal clear—pun intended—that these beads are different."

His gold eyes bored into mine for a beat too long. Under the right circumstances, say a full moon for instance, I could stare into those gold eyes all night, but not in a room full of my peers meditating and with a wicked hangover. I shifted uncomfortably. The movement snapped him out of his daze.

"To answer your question, the bowl is made of selenite. It allows the beads to constantly charge and recharge until they are removed from it." He dipped his chin toward the bowl. "Close your eyes and take one."

I raised an eyebrow. "You're not going to try anything, are you?"

He pressed his lips together. Either his subtle way of telling me to shut up, or I had struck a chord. Based on the way he stared at me, I was leaning toward the latter. Not that I was complaining or anything.

"Fine." I closed my eyes and stuck my left hand inside. I felt around the bowl. Occasionally a strand of beads would feel okay but not quite right. Though if someone asked me what "right" felt like, I wouldn't be able to put it into words. It was more of a feeling. A gut instinct. I worked with crystals a lot. Even wore a necklace that had a quartz crystal pendant with turquoise wrapped around it. It grounded me when life got dicey. I never left home without it, and when I didn't have it? Well, I don't like reliving that time.

Suddenly, something triggered in me, and my hand wrapped around a strand. As I brought it up, it clung to my hand, as if unwilling to release me.

"Interesting," Hunky whispered.

My attention shot over to him, but this time his gold eyes were glued to the pagan prayer bead strand. I felt strangely protective of it and pulled it to my chest. "What is?"

"Well, that particular prayer bead represents Lilith, which, given your affiliation with her, isn't surprising." He nodded at the Air symbol on my left hand. "However, it's made with crystals that aren't typically used in association with her. I've had it in my possession for a very long time."

I studied the beaded strand. An owl charm hung from one end of it, definitely representing Lilith. A pentagram with a circle around it hung from the other end. Small silver spacers separated each of the crystals. There was a disproportionate number of yellow beads compared to the other elemental colors, but each element was represented.

"The element beads are variations of calcite. Solid representation and a good conductor."

"Hmmm." My fingers trailed along the round calcite beads to the gorgeous, oddly shaped red stones. I pulled the strand closer, studying them. They reminded me of blood but not the one-dimensional variety of a blood bag; more of a representation of the living, breathing lifeblood of a human.

"Red jasper."

"It's beautiful," I murmured.

KB ANNE

"It is very multidimensional. If you look closer, you'll see the veins of different colors of red. Reminds me of blood pumping."

I swallowed as his neck stretched in front of my mouth with his carotid artery pulsing. His unique smell tantalized me. My fangs descended. I closed my eyes to push them back. I had control of my bloodlust most of the time, but Hunky tested my control, whether he realized it or not.

My fingers found three irregular blue stones, then three round iridescent white ones.

"Azurite is the blue, and moonstone is the white."

"It reminds me of the moon. There are so many dimensions to each of them. The azurite is beautiful too. Reminds me of the sky. Why aren't the crystals commonly used to represent Lilith?"

"Red jasper is because of the red tone—Queen of Vampires and all that."

"Right."

"But it pulses with energy and is multidimensional. Like vampires, it's not defined by one thing."

I pulled my lips into my mouth.

"Azurite represents the energy of inner strength and allows balancing of emotions. It's typically combined with malachite, so alone it resembles the sky, and it's usually used as a Heavenly stone aligned with Rhiannon, but Lilith reminds me of Heaven too."

I swallowed. She felt heavenly to me as well. Hunky set the bar for raw masculinity, but he didn't fear sharing his sensitive side either.

"Moonstone is conducive to inner clarity when one is confused or having a difficult time concentrating." He winked at me. "It is a symbol of light and hope with an intense connection to the feminine—thus why I chose moonstone as one of Lilith's crystals."

"Chose, as in, you made this strand?"

"Chose, as in, I made all the strands."

I studied the strand closely. "Really?"

"You believe I'm incapable of creating such fine beadwork?"

"Well, yes."

"Because I'm a man."

"Well, yeah."

"That's awfully closed-minded of you. That would be the equivalent of me saying that you cannot be a slayer of evil supernaturals because you're a woman."

I cleared my throat. "Point taken."

"The Brotherhood encourages more than brute force to achieve their end. Craftmanship, metalworking, meditation."

I rolled my eyes at the mention of the last one. I couldn't help it.

He pushed himself off the floor and stood. "Class dismissed. We will try again the day after tomorrow. Same time, same place, with less conversation and more focus."

His gold eyes pinned me in place, and I sat immobilized while the rest of the class left. When the door swung shut, the spell or compellation, or whatever he cast over me, was broken.

"What the hell? Are you trying to get me alone?" I growled, feeling an invasion of my control. I was tempted to throw an accusation of violating Silverwood Academy rules in his face.

He smirked at me.

His freaking sexy face.

"Whatever," I said, clutching the strand as I walked

toward the door. I stopped and glanced over my shoulder. His gold eyes met mine as if he had been watching me, and more than as his student. "Thank you for the beads. I'll focus on them tonight and see if you visit me in my dreams."

His lips turned down. "Do not mistake the gift of the pagan prayer beads as anything more. I am your guide, and you are my student. That is all."

"You can say whatever you want if it helps you sleep at night, but I know better," I yelled over my shoulder and strode away.

Challenge accepted.

CHAPTER

TWELVE

C^{yn}

MUSCLES in my body ached that I didn't know I had. That I didn't know existed. I'd never been so sore or sweaty in my entire life. I was the student who got by in gym class by doing just enough to earn participation points each day but never doing enough to break a sweat. Hells, during the weight-lifting unit, I used the lowest setting, pretending to huff and puff like I struggled with it. My performances were worthy of an Emmy but only I knew the truth. I didn't even trust my friends, Marie and Callie with that information, because they were try-hards. They assumed I was weak and pathetic when it came to athletics, and they were too busy competing against each other to concern themselves with me anyway, but as I climbed the dungeon stairs with Anastasia after class, I regretted my past gross neglect of physical activity.

"I thought vampires were supposed to be superfast and physically gifted," I complained as I willed my leg to rise to the next step.

She laughed. "They are, but Professor Bladecroft worked us hard."

I scowled at her. "How are you not crying? You're just a witch. Unless witches are physically advanced too."

She winked at me. "Witches are naturally athletic."

"I hate you."

She laughed and raised her hand to my shoulder to stop me. "Remember, I *am* a witch. I whipped up a little spell to lift the fatigue."

"Bitch," I hissed as I broke free from her hold to take the next step.

She caught up to me, practically hopping up and down. I wanted to throat-punch her, now that I knew how.

"I could do it for you too, you know."

I stopped. "You can?"

"All I need is your permission. Don't forget rule number one."

Memories of my time in Silverwood Prison when I had feasted on the wolf shifter came back to me. I didn't even know I could compel people, but my inner vamp did. "How could I forget that one?"

"Good. Now, stand still."

"Not a problem."

She murmured a few lines as she wiggled her fingers and pointed at me. A hot breeze touched my face and wrapped itself around my body. Tingles ran from my fingertips down to my tippy toes and back up to the top of my head. The muscle ache disappeared as the tingles left my body and evaporated into the air. I blinked, feeling refreshed, alive, and ready to kick more ass.

"Wow! I feel great."

She winked again. "Stick with me, kid. We're going places together."

"Gladly."

"Stupid witchy magick," someone snarled from the bottom of the stairs.

We both turned around and saw Azalea all by herself, glaring at us.

"I could do it for you too," Anastasia offered. "All you need to do is ask, but you have to ask nicely."

Azalea glared at her. "Never. Pain reminds us what we went through to get here."

Her judgement curled up the stairwell and hit me square in the chest, igniting fire inside me. "I know exactly what I went through to get here, and if Anastasia can alleviate it with a little magick, so be it."

"Figures you'd want it. Vampires are weak. There's a reason their population is so low. They're always the first to go rogue. To join the dark forces."

"What is this a *Star Wars* episode? You dare use such an antiquated term in this school?" Anastasia asked.

"You know it's true. You're just trying to protect her."

Anastasia threw her hand down. A puff of magick encircled us, muffling the stairwell noises. She tugged my arm and began to climb. "Let's go, Cyn. We don't need that negative energy in our lives."

She almost ran up the rest of the stairs. I managed to keep up with her, which was an impressive feat for me, considering the wrecked state I was in moments ago. Anastasia's spell was potent stuff. But instead of relishing in feeling like a normal person again—well, I guess I'd never feel like a normal human person again, so a normal supernatural—I was preoccupied with Azalea's comments. Anastasia had blown her off by making a joke reference to *Star Wars*, but I knew the evil existed, and so did Maleficium—the correct term for dark magick—and sometimes they combined together, joining forces for malicious reasons. I hadn't grown up in the supernatural world, but I wasn't stupid.

I grabbed Anastasia's bicep. "Red, what did Azalea mean about vampires turning evil? Why are their populations so low?"

She waved her hand, blowing it off. "Don't worry about Azalea. Haters gonna hate."

I squeezed a little harder than I intended.

"Ouch, Cyn, you're hurting me."

I loosened my grip but leaned closer to her. "What does she mean, Red?"

She refused to look at me. "Nothing. Don't worry about her."

"Why won't you look at me?"

A shock of electricity shot through my fingers, and I released my hold on her.

"Because you're a vampire, okay? A Sempiternal—the most powerful kind. You can compel anyone just by looking at them, and I'm not wearing vervain. I don't want you to compel me."

I blinked. "I didn't realize."

She pursed her lips, breathing in and out of her nose. "No, of course you didn't. You're new. You're still learning how to control yourself and your urges, but I won't be compelled." Her eyes watered. She blinked rapidly to stop the flow.

"Did I hurt you?"

"No, you didn't, but I've lost family to rogue vampires. Vampires and witches have a long, complicated history.

Some good. Some bad. Some light. Some dark. Some twisted."

My eyes watered too. "I didn't know. I won't bother you again." I hurried away.

Vamp speed was a real thing. Within seconds I darted down a dark hallway and rested against the wall, my chest heaving but not from exhaustion. The day Dez turned me, she had issued my death warrant. I was a bloodthirsty, evil person who couldn't be trusted.

"Hey, is someone down there?" a male voice called out.

I immediately quieted and squinted down the hallway. I could just make out broad shoulders, a tall frame, and a mile-long jawline. But the thing that really got me was the pulsing carotid artery and an overwhelming thirst that flooded my veins.

I swallowed the salvia pooling in my mouth as I tried to fight my canines from descending.

"Hello?" he called out again. The timbre of his baritone played to parts of my body that hadn't been attended to since before Derrick dumped me (and even then, not so much).

"I'm here," I whispered in a seductive tone I didn't recognize. I slapped my hand over my mouth. What the hells was that?

Footsteps echoed down the hall. As he approached, my nose tingled. Notes of mint and cedarwood filled the air, along with the tangy musk of blood.

He was close enough that I could clearly see him, but he didn't seem to be aware of me. I knew that every supernatural was blessed with different abilities, but he should at least have been able to see me. And why did his blood smell different than the blood of all the other supes I'd met?

He crept closer. His green eyes almost shined in the

darkness, but that didn't seem to aid his eyesight at all. Then it hit me why he was different than the other supes I'd met. He wasn't a supe at all. Fear raced through me. My hands clutched the wall behind me, my nails digging in. What was a human doing here?

"Hello?" he called out. "Anyone there?"

Before I could stop myself, I appeared in front of him. "Hi," I whispered in that same low, seductive voice. I stared into those green eyes, my mouth watering at the delicious scent of his blood. My fingers trailed along his neck and wrapped around his head. His shoulder muscles tensed, as he tried to resist me. "Just relax."

He followed my instructions beautifully. My lips curled, revealing my fangs.

"Hold still."

And I bit into his neck.

THIRTEEN

D^{ez}

MY LEATHER PANTS rocked as I walked down the hallway to Demonology class. Cyn wouldn't regret wearing them for Weapons Training. Wish I'd had Weapons Training instead of Meditation. Hunky had been a lovely distraction, but I still didn't understand the practicality of meditating. It wouldn't save me in battle. Learning the proper mechanics of swinging a sword would. I stalked down the hall to Demonology. Contrary to popular belief, not all demons were inherently evil. Some chose darkness over light, but that didn't mean they wanted to recruit or kill every supernatural and human who came along their path. Dad had worked with a few over the years. He suspected one of the top leaders of the Children of the Sun organization was a greater demon. Those were always evil.

I plunged my hand into my pocket and played with the

prayer beads again. I'd never admit it to Hunky, but they did settle me long enough to sit through Spiritual Alchemy. That professor liked to talk. A lot. And I wasn't much for listening. I preferred action over words, which is why meditation wouldn't work for me. No one should expect me to lie still and quiet my mind and think of nothing when Dad's killer was on the loose. I needed tools to equip me to catch the bastard, not count backward from ten and enter the imaginary green meadow. The beads, however, kept my fingers busy.

Goddess, please let Demonology include physical activity. I couldn't take another minute in a chair, listening to some old chap talk.

"Lilith, right?" Someone knocked her elbow into my side by way of a greeting.

I grabbed her arm and pinned it behind her back. "Touch me again and I will break you."

The tall blond cowered in my presence. "I . . . I meant no disrespect. The opposite, actually. Anyone who can pull daggers out of thin air and stick them into a windstorm is someone I'd like to know. I'm a fan."

I stared up at her. Her eyes were an almost unnatural shade of blue. I tightened my grip to serve as a warning before I shoved her away. She wobbled, her arms and legs flailing as she tried to keep her balance. I caught her arm before she landed on her ass.

"Siren?"

She straightened. "How can you tell?"

"It was either that or a mermaid, and I harpooned the last mermaid I met."

"You killed Suzie?"

I flared my arms and chest out to demonstrate that I could take her too if needed. A siren wasn't as much of a threat out of the water without her true voice, but she could still be difficult to dispatch. "Got a problem with that?"

She narrowed her eyes, her muscles in her arms tightening. Then she laughed and her whole body loosened. "Naw, I'm just playing with you. That bitch deserved a spear to her heart. She was a good lay, though."

I started walking to class again. "How do you think I got into her lair?"

"Nice." She raised her large hand for a high five, which I gave. I was feeling charitable. Must have been something in the air. Plus, the siren had kicked serious ass during the Induction Ceremony. She deserved my respect too, though she seemed less intimidating today than last night. Maybe she'd had a rough night with her goddess like my night with Lilith.

I glanced at the Water emblem on her navy-blue tank top. "Morrigan, right?"

"Yeah. Nice pants." She pointed to mine, then hers, which were the same leather but red.

"You've got good taste."

"Hell yeah, I do." We high-fived again like it was the most natural thing to do in the entire world.

"Alyze," she said in a deep voice.

"Dez," I replied.

She pulled open the giant wood door. "Ever kill a demon before?"

"Five. But I've worked with a few too, so I'm not anti-demon. I'm anti-asshole."

Alyze grinned at me, her bright blue eyes flashing with excitement. "Dez, I think we've got the makings of a great friendship."

"If you show me how you did that move with Water last night, I'll consider it."

She threw back her head and laughed. "Fair, but only if you show me how to pull daggers out of thin air."

I frowned as I walked past her. "The windstorm had hundreds of them. Maybe thousands. I yanked two out. And I didn't make it out unharmed." I showed her the slice on my upper arm that wasn't fully healed yet, even with my accelerated healing.

"It wasn't just wind for you?"

"Clearly not."

She grabbed my arm without asking, but I didn't hammer kick her since we were sorta friends now. She bent her head, studying it.

"Wow." Her blue eyes flashed as they met mine. "May I?"

"Sure, go for it."

She closed her eyes and murmured a spell. Her hands warmed, and healing energy swirled in and around the wound until any remnants of the injury were gone. When she was finished, she examined the wound and smiled, satisfied with her work.

"Thanks. I didn't know sirens could conduct magick outside of the water."

Her lips turned down, and her shoulders drooped, withdrawing back into herself. "Most don't. That's why my parents made me come here. I didn't fit in."

I slapped her on the back. "Welcome to the club, sister. I never fit in anywhere."

Her face lit up. She really was one of the most beautiful creatures I'd ever met.

Her lip rose in a devilish grin. "Did we just become best friends?"

I laughed, shaking my head. "I think so. Let's go learn about demons."

She swaggered past me. "You know how to talk so nice."

I smiled to myself. I'd made a friend that wasn't related to me. Sometimes, I amazed myself.

The classroom gave off old-world library vibes and reminded me of the bunker's library. I'd spent much of my youth wandering through the dusty tomes, learning about the differences between each of the supernatural species and their vulnerabilities, along with thousands of other tips I stored in the back of my mind until I needed them. I'd also delved into the occasional romance novel, fantasizing about bringing those scenes to life one day. Perhaps Hunky would volunteer as tribute . . .

Alyze snapped her fingers in front of my face. "Oh Dezireee."

I blinked back to the present. "Sorry. This classroom reminds me of a place I used to hang out at."

She glanced around, taking in the shelves loaded with skulls, the glass jars filled with eyeballs, miscellaneous animal parts, and various insects suspended in some type of gel, and other strange and unusual items. "Willingly?"

I snorted. "Well, that depended on the cause."

When I didn't expand on my explanation, she raised an eyebrow, nodding her head like, *Go on*.

But I never got the chance. Out of the corner of my eye, I caught a large stack of books weaving through the desks, as well as, the fast approaching vampire in the opposite direction, along with the impending collision.

A loud growl ripped through the room as books flew in every direction. Rather than crash to the floor, though, the books stopped and hovered in the air before returning back to the towering stack someone was carrying. The vamp—a tall glass of dark and handsome—spun around to face the book-bearing individual he'd knocked into. I got a full display of tight ass and miles of bulging back muscles.

"Why, helloooo," I purred, knowing at least one of my fantasies would come true later.

"Watch where you're going," he grunted to the book-pile carrier who he'd barreled into seconds ago.

A small head peered around the side of the pile. I blinked a few times, unable to believe my eyes.

Holy shit. That wasn't just some kid carrying around a too-tall stack of books. That was Alexander Logan, famed demon hunter. His battle stories were legend among supernaturals. I'd been privileged enough to be left in his care for a short stint when I was seven. No way, he'd remember me.

The stack of books rose into the air once more, glided over our heads, and landed on a table at the front of the class.

"I . . ." Steamy stuttered. "I . . ." He swallowed. "I'm sorry for yelling at you."

Actually he'd growled at him, but whatever.

Alexander Logan tipped his head. "Apology accepted. But," he pointed a finger at Steamy, "watch where you're going, and always be wary of who you attack."

Steamy shuffled backward, shoving his hands into his pockets. "I wasn't going to fight."

Alexander Logan smirked at him. "You were, but perhaps you've learned your first lesson in Demonology."

Steamy shook his head and backed into my seat. I cradled his hips. "Careful there, big guy."

He spun around and eyed me. "S-s-s-sorry," he muttered and fled the scene by sliding into the nearest available seat.

Alexander Logan straightened his bow tie, strode to the

front of the class, climbed onto the raised stage, then turned around to face us.

"Good evening. I am Alexander Logan, your Demonology professor," he said in the same thick Ukrainian accent I remembered from my childhood.

"What?!?!" I shouted, flinging my hands out in front of me.

"Miss Deziree, I see you haven't forgotten me."

I gasped, unable to believe that he remembered me.

Murmurings of surprise from the surrounding students filled the room, including from Steamy, but I only had eyes for the man who had taught me how to sniff out a demon by using himself as bait.

"Tonight we will leap right into a lesson on defensive spells against demons with myself serving as your demon."

Every jaw in the room dropped. Alexander Logan was known throughout our world as the most prolific demon hunter, but few knew he was one too. After all, the best way to catch a demon was to be one.

"Any volunteers?"

Discontented energy seeped off my classmates. To this day, prejudices against demons continued to persist, regardless of Alexander Logan's efforts or any of his other less famous contemporaries, but I wasn't afraid of him. Not of the man who had watched an annoying, precocious seven-year-old while her dad recovered at Silverwood Hospital from injuries received after a Children of the Sun ambush. He had been lucky to get out alive that time.

My hand shot up.

"Miss Deziree," he said.

I smiled to myself, excitement surging through me.

"Be careful," Alyze whispered.

I raised my eyebrow, surprised a gay siren harbored prejudice against demons.

"He's powerful, even underwater, so disable his hands as quickly as possible."

I sighed, relieved my new friend—my only friend—wasn't anti-demon. She was just familiar with his reputation too.

I already knew that tidbit. Alexander Logan had taught it to me himself. I walked onto the stage with my chest flared. Fake it till you make it. Never let them think you're scared of them. The man standing before me had taught me that.

He turned his back to the class and winked at me. "Nice to see you, Dez."

"I didn't think you'd remember me."

"How could I forget the little hunter who nagged me to teach her everything I knew?"

I shrugged. "You've been busy since then."

"Yes," he laughed, "yes, I have, but I'd never forget you. You made quite an impression on me, and your dad ... well, he was one of my most trusted friends. And as you well know, those are few and far between, but we'll talk later. For now, I want you to take a hit. Several, actually, without fighting."

I straightened, surprised he'd warned me of his intentions and nervous because his spells had knocked much stronger supernaturals than me on their asses. Plus, I wasn't very good with defensive magick.

He winked, then turned around.

"A Sempiternal mimics the energy of a demon in several respects."

I frowned, wondering why he was sharing things about my nature with the rest of the class. It wasn't like I hid behind my powers and abilities, but I didn't want everyone else knowing my business. And strengths and weaknesses of supernaturals would be covered in Elemental History, not Demonology.

"In order to disable a demon, you must catch them unaware."

He sliced his hand in the air. A gust of wind slammed into my chest.

"Ooof," I grunted through clenched teeth, doubling over. That hurt.

Something deep inside me woke up. Incredible power surged through my body, wanting to defend against this attack, but I held it back. I promised I'd take whatever he sent at me.

"Fire confounds and confuses," he said, raising his palms. Fireballs formed on them. Realizing what he planned to do, I closed my eyes and grounded myself, envisioning a light coating of armor around me. I felt the fireballs hit me and explode against my armor. I screamed, acting as if the flames hurt, and I flailed around like he used to do when I shot him with my little fireballs. I stilled, remembering that I'd once been able to shoot fireballs and control flame, but something had happened. I couldn't do it anymore.

"Water encapsulates," he shouted, flinging his hands in the air as if he were a conductor for an orchestra. I remained still, heat vibrating off my skin, ready to douse the water. I let it encircle me, knowing I could break free whenever I wanted.

"And, finally, Earth captures," he yelled, stomping his foot. A crack rippled out from him, getting wider and wider. Power bloomed in my chest, and I knew that if I wanted to, I could break free, but Alexander Logan had told me to take a hit, and I trusted him. My body pulsed with raw energy. My canines descended. I bit my lip, sweet liquid filling my mouth, distracting me from fighting the elements he pummeled at me. I pinched my eyes shut, avoiding the battle fury pulsing beneath the surface of my skin.

He clapped his hands, and the elements disappeared, leaving me standing there with clenched fists and tears streaming down my face.

"Thank you for volunteering, Miss Deziree. You may return to your seat." As I walked across the stage to the stairs, he said, "Class, split into pairs, and attempt to cast a spell with your strongest element at your opponent."

He turned to me and murmured, "Come see me after class."

Oh, I intended to.

FOURTEEN

C^{yn}

GUILT ATE AT ME. I'd broken two of the three Silverwood Academy rules. The only one I hadn't broken was the one about stabbing another classmate in the back, and if I had a stake, there was a good chance I might have broken that one too. I didn't know if my victim was a student at the Academy or not, but if he wasn't, what was he doing wandering down dark hallways in a school for newly turned supernaturals? Individuals who could drain them of their blood, twist their head off, or compel them to forget that they'd even met you.

At least I didn't kill him. There was that. But it didn't make me feel any less awful about what I'd done. Afterward, I vamp-sped to my room and buried myself under blankets until I had the courage (and sense) to check my appearance in the mirror to ensure my chin wasn't covered in blood. It wasn't, by the way. Apparently I was a clean bloodsucker. But I felt sick and twisted all the same. Azalea was right. I was a monster. A beast who, given the right motivation, would turn evil. I was better off getting staked now rather than taking an innocent life later. I couldn't be trusted.

With firm resolution, I pushed myself off the bed. I'd find Lilith or the headmistress— I stopped. Was there a headmistress? Did Mother Earth hang out at some desk, listening to student complaints and such? I shook my head. It didn't matter. I'd find someone in charge, share my actions with them, and accept my punishment, most likely ending this life as unpoetically as I'd entered it. I swung open the door, bound and determined to confess my sins, and came face-to-face with the very person I wanted to forget.

His green eyes widened. His fisted hand dropped to his side as if he'd raised it to knock. "Uh, hi. I didn't mean to startle you."

The timbre in his voice struck my lady bits again, as did the scent of his musky human blood. I stepped back into my room, putting distance between us. There was no way he'd remember me. I wasn't exactly sure how compellation worked, but it had been so dark in that hallway that he'd never guess it was me.

My eyes skimmed over the tiny pinpricks at his throat.

"Oh, that," he said, his fingers skimming over them. "I got bit by something. Marks are almost gone now."

I nodded, afraid my voice would betray me.

He scratched it. "Anastasia put some ointment on it, but it still itches a little."

Crap. Anastasia. She probably saw me biting him in a vision and told him where he could confront me. I thought she was my friend. Showed what I knew. I had stopped trusting the girls in high school, so why should it be any different with the women at the Academy?

He leaned forward. "Are you okay?"

I swiped an errant tear. It was time to face the music—er, my victim. I was on my way to confess my crime anyway. My eyes met his. "I'm fine. Can I help you with something?"

His green eyes stared at me for a few uncomfortable beats before he blinked, and pink rushed into his cheeks. "I'm sorry. This might sound like the cheesiest line you've ever heard, but has anyone ever told you, your eyes are mesmerizing? They remind me of fluorite."

"Fluorite? As in the crystal?"

His red lips rose into a smile, the color of them much too close to a cherry Blow Pop, my favorite flavor. I licked my lips.

How about a blow? a lusty voice said in my head. The same one I'd used to compel him earlier. It took every ounce of my control not to groan. From annoyance or pleasure—I couldn't tell which. I pinned my lips together to prevent any more inappropriate things from coming out of my mouth.

He tracked the movement before he blinked again. "Yes, as in the crystal. Fluorite encourages openness to new adventures. It assists in removing feelings of guilt and turmoil and allows making changes to clearer pathways." He leaned closer, staring into my eyes, his carotid artery pulsing near my closed lips. "The hints of purple suggest you embrace your magickal side."

I swallowed the lump in my throat. His musky scent filled my nostrils, and this time, I didn't want to suck his blood. I wanted to see if his lips tasted as good as they looked. A breath width was all the existed between us. We blinked at the same time, breaking the spell, and inched away from each other to an acceptable distance.

"My name's Canyon."

"Canyon as in the geological feature?"

He smiled. "Hello, fellow science nerd. Finally, I've met my people, because I don't know if you can tell or not, but I'm completely human. One of the only ones at the Academy."

I wanted to say, *Yes, I realized that when I bit into your neck and your blood drove me to want to drain you.* However, I went with a safer alternative. Which I blurted out before I could stop myself.

"Why are you allowed to attend?" Then, realizing my rudeness, I quickly rephrased. "I thought the Academy was for supernaturals."

His cheeks reddened again. I never realized I had such an effect on men. I rather enjoyed it.

"My mom is one of the professors here."

As if that explained everything. My forehead pinched.

"She's a turned vampire, as opposed to a born one who changes when they come of age."

Dez had never explained all the aspects of vampirism to me. According to my sister, I would have changed into a vampire in the future, but she had rushed the process by killing me. So, what did that make me? A turned vampire or a born one? I looped my arm in his and walked out into the hall. "Tell me more about your mom becoming a vampire."

He stiffened. I might have overstepped with my forwardness.

"Sorry," I said. "Just thought we'd go for a stroll."

He grinned at me as he patted my hand. "Just shocked is all. Mom always warns me to be wary of supes, especially newly turned vampires, but you seem harmless."

Oh, Canyon. Why did the pretty ones have to be so stupid?

"So, about your mom?"

"Right. She actually sent me to get you. You missed class today, and she was worried you'd gone astray on your first day."

She wasn't wrong, especially if she'd seen the tiny pinpricks on her son's neck. But then, why would she send her son to find me? Was this a setup? I stopped walking, and my hand slipped from his arm.

He stepped toward me, invading my personal space again. "What's wrong?"

"Just feeling overwhelmed. I think I'll go lie down again."

He took my left hand and cradled it in his. "Why do I feel so drawn to you?"

I stepped back. "Must be a vamp thing. You don't even know me."

He closed the distance between us. "But I want to."

"Everything okay here?" Dez asked from behind me before placing herself between us.

Canyon backed away from her. Everything about my sister promised violence and pain at the slightest provocation. A predator to the core.

"And you are . . . ?" she said.

"Canyon. I'm a friend of Cynda's."

She cocked her head, staring at me. "I didn't realize Cyn had any friends."

I raised my chin in defiance. I wasn't about to let her

intimidate me. "You'd be surprised, Sister. People actually like me."

Her eyes pivoted to the bite marks on Canyon's neck. "I bet."

Heat rose to my cheeks. If she sold me out, a stake to my heart was a real possibility. Of course, I'd been ready to die just a short time ago. Now, not so much.

"Cynda didn't come to class today, so I wanted to check on her."

Dez tilted her head in my direction. "She didn't?"

My sister's purple eyes scanned me, and her forehead pinched in what appeared to be concern.

"I wasn't feeling well. I'm better now. Canyon and I were just going to go for a walk."

Her attention shifted back to Canyon. "Where were you going?"

"I was taking her to my mom."

His pupils pulsed in and out. Was Dez compelling him? "Who, pray tell, is your mom?"

"Professor Goldwell. She teaches Ghostbusting."

"Huh. With a name like that, I'd expect her to teach Spiritual Alchemy."

"She isn't a witch or proficient in those areas. She's a turned vampire."

"You don't say . . ." She turned her purple eyes on me. If she thought she could compel me to say or do something, she had another thing coming.

"Canyon, we should get going."

He scratched his neck, drawing attention to the bite marks again. They were fading by the second, but not fast enough for my sister's hawk eyes.

"Are you sure you're up to it?" he asked. "You just said you wanted to lie down again."

Dez raised a carefully manicured eyebrow at me.

Confidence surged in me. "I suddenly feel better. Must be the company." I stepped around my sister and walked down the hall. Canyon soon joined me.

"Oh, Cyn," my sister called out in her singsong voice. "Got a second to speak in private?"

I groaned, and this time there was no question the cause of it. "Yes. Wait for me, please?"

Canyon nodded. "Yeah, sure."

I hurried back into our room so Dez wouldn't try to embarrass me in the hall. She entered, slamming the door behind her.

"May I remind you what the rules are?" she hissed.

I raised my chin. I would not let my older, taller, and pushier sister intimidate me. "I know exactly what the rules are."

"Do you? Because from the fading marks on the boytoy's neck, it suggests you don't."

"Those aren't from me."

"Really? Should I go ask the ephemeral?"

I narrowed my eyes at her. I wasn't exactly sure what an ephemeral was, but the way she said it made me suspect it was a not-nice term for humans.

"By compelling? Isn't that a violation of one of the Academy rules you hurl around like accusations?"

She stepped toward me. I didn't back down. You can't with a predator. "I didn't compel him."

"Then what was the pupil-dilation thing?"

She surprised me by scratching her ear as she sat on the bed. "Huh. I didn't think I did. I don't have a lot of experience with ephemerals."

Never had I witnessed my sister so unsure and, dare I say, vulnerable. I almost sat beside her to comfort her.

Almost, but she had pissed me off, and I still hadn't forgiven her.

"Why don't you take some time to figure your shit out before you accuse me of rule violation," I growled, leaving her to fester.

CHAPTER
FIFTEEN

D^{ez}

M<small>Y SISTER WAS HEADED</small> down a dangerous path. Biting a professor's son? That could lead to automatic suspension—or worse, a stake through the heart. And as much as my sister drove me crazy with her emerging independent spirit, I wanted to keep her close, especially after what Alexander Logan told me after Demonology. The reason he wanted me to take a hit from him—four hits actually—was to test whether I still possessed abilities to repel and counteract elemental magick. From my classmates' point of view, Professor Logan had pummeled me with elemental magick, and I had been at his mercy until he released me. But that wasn't what had actually happened. Long-suppressed powers rose within me, longing to unleash themselves. I'd kept that hidden from my classmates, and after class he'd warned me to continue to do so. No one could find out what I could do.

I had asked him if Cyn possessed the same powers as me, but he didn't know. He planned to observe her in his class over the next few weeks.

I pulled the pagan prayer beads out of my pocket. After Hunky gave them to me, I found it easier to concentrate in my other classes. I didn't know if it had anything to do with the crystals or if it was because the more physical classes kept me occupied, but whatever the case, my day had gone far more smoothly than I expected. Well, until my sister had f'ed it up because she couldn't keep her fangs out of a boy's neck. She had good taste though. In addition to smelling positively scrumptious, he was a juicy piece of manflesh almost as delicious as my Meditation instructor. Almost.

My fingers trailed along the beads, spacers, and charms. I pulled the strand closer, studying it. A lot of fine work had been involved in making the prayer bead strands. I'd been too hungover this morning to fully appreciate it.

Thoughts and ideas raced in and out of my mind as I ran my fingers up and down the prayer beads, mulling over my conversation with Professor Logan. I didn't completely understand why I had hide my abilities, but I trusted Alexander Logan. Something else kept needling at me, though. I left the room in search of answers.

When I entered the dark hallway, I glanced up at the ceiling. It was much later than I thought. My Astrology professor had said the stars on the ceiling changed according to their actual movement in the night sky. Of course, indoors it was always a cloudless night in order for the stars to cast enough light in the hallway for us to see. I hurried down the hall, took a left, and skidded to a stop.

"Fast reflexes, Deziree," Hunky said, his voice doing things to me that weren't legal.

"Why are you out wandering the halls?" My question came out more accusatory that I intended.

"I could ask you the same."

His quick counter response caught me off guard. He made my mind a jumbled mess. I shook my head to clear it, because he was actually the person I was looking for.

"I wanted to ask you a question."

"So, it was kismet we found each other. I wanted to check to see how the prayer beads were working out for you."

I edged closer. "You could have asked me tomorrow during class."

His eyes sparkled with mischief. "Now, what fun would that be?"

I hooked my fingers around his shirt collar. "I knew I was right."

He squeezed my hands as he gently removed them and put distance between us. "I'm not sure what you're referring to, but we don't have class on Tuesdays. I wanted to ensure your concentration improved."

I narrowed my eyes at him. What game was he playing? His actions and words were contradictions to each other.

He watched me as he said, "Good evening, Professor Goldwell."

A short woman sporting a blond bob appeared behind him.

"Good evening, Jace. How did your first day go?"

Jace. Even his name was sexy.

A delicious dimple popped up on his cheek that disappeared just as quickly as he turned to face her. "Very well. I was just checking on one of my students to ensure she kept up with her meditations."

Professor Goldwell's gaze landed on me. Red rimmed her eyes, and I knew at once what she was. A turned vampire with her bloodlust barely under control. My hunter instincts snapped to full alert. My fingers itched for a stake.

"Hello, I'm Dez. I believe my sister, Cyn, is in your class."

Her lips turned down as if she tasted something foul.

"Cyn and Dezire. How appropriate for vampires who reek of sex and lust," she snapped.

A fire ignited inside me. If it was a fight she wanted, I'd deliver. "Excuse me?"

Jace stepped between us, his chest flaring out, his arm muscles tightening. "Professor Goldwell, that is inappropriate."

More red filled her eyes. "Is it? Or is it inappropriate that you are out in the hallway after hours with a student?"

"I . . . I . . ." he stammered.

"First of all, Miss Bitch, I'm twenty-two, and I might be a student here, but there are no 'after hours' at the Academy. We are two consenting adults, and what we decide to do or not do is none of your business."

"How dare you," she started.

I threw up my left palm. "How dare I? How dare you."

Her eyes narrowed at my raised hand. "Oh, you're one of *hers*."

My Air element mark. Oops, forgot about that. But I didn't like how she said "*hers*." Not one bit. No one dissed on Lilith.

I opened my mouth, about to let loose on Goldipants

and her closed-minded views, when Lilith strolled up behind her.

"Goldilocks, were you bragging about me to my initiates again?"

Goldipants's face paled. I smiled to myself. Can anyone say, busted?

"I . . . I . . ." She shifted uncomfortably. Good. Served the bitch right for bashing my goddess.

Easy, Lilith said in my head. *Let me handle it.*

"Jace, dear, would you mind if Professor Goldwell and I spoke alone for a few minutes? Could you take Dez outside?"

"Sh-sh-sure." But he stood there awestruck, dumbstruck . . . I couldn't tell which.

"Come on." I grabbed his bicep and yanked him down the hall and out the nearest door.

As soon as the cool night air hit his face, he drew in a deep breath. "That was Lilith, Goddess of Night, Queen of Vampires."

I laughed. "I know who she is. Someone has a serious crush on her."

My comment snapped him out of his revelry. "I don't have a crush on her. She's a goddess, for gods' sake. Aren't you a little awestruck by her?"

I shrugged. "I guess. We've hung out a lot since she selected me. Plus, my wicked hangover from this morning was all her fault."

He grabbed my arms. "You've seen her outside of the Induction Ceremony?"

I tried to pull away, but he was surprisingly strong. Well, not completely surprising because of those big, thick, yummy biceps, but still, I beat most supernaturals in the

KB ANNE

raw strength department. "Uh, yeah. You already knew she selected me."

He took a deep breath in and out. "I was aware, but it's not common for the goddesses to socialize with their initiates after the Induction Ceremony."

"Well, that's not the case with Lilith. She visited me in the morning, gave me those dark sunglasses you made me remove. She even ate breakfast with us."

He raised an eyebrow. "Anyone else see her?"

What in the hells was his problem? "Duh, yes. All of us."

He shook his head. "No, that's impossible. Think, Dez. Has anyone else actually seen her?"

He seemed really sincere about it, and stubborn. Definitely stubborn.

"My sister."

"Anyone else?"

"What's the big deal?"

He looked around, as if checking to see if we were being followed. His nostrils flared in and out, scenting the air. A low growl erupted from his chest before he snagged my hand and dragged me under the cover of an oak tree. He pushed me against it abruptly. Roughly. I liked it. He pressed into me, the hard lines of his chest pushing against my firm, soft mounds, my nipples hard as rocks. He slipped his hands around my waist, his fingers finding exposed skin on my back. I hissed in pleasure and wrapped my hands around his broad shoulders, my body curling around him. "I like a man who knows what he wants, but weren't you the one who insisted we couldn't be together?"

"We aren't," he breathed into my ear, his hot breath tickling every part of me in the best of ways. "Now, listen closely. Stay away from Professor Goldwell."

"That I figured out on my own. But what about Cynda? She has class with her."

"I'll get her schedule changed."

"Is my sister in danger?"

He pressed harder against me, his nose trailing along my jaw back to my ear. "Yes."

I froze. I had just gotten my sister back, and now she was in danger? An intense desire to protect her and eliminate anyone who even looked at her sideways filled me. Power surged below the surface. My fangs elongated. "I'll kill her."

He squeezed me in his vise-like arms. "You can't. Not yet."

Not yet meant I would one day get to. But I liked deadlines. Get it? Dead lines? "When?"

"Act cool, keep quiet about your interactions with Lilith, and stay away from Goldwell."

"And if I don't?"

His hand grabbed my chin, his gold eyes spearing into mine, his lips tantalizingly close. "You will."

Instead of arguing with him, I switched tactics and pressed my lips into his, my tongue darting into his mouth. His body stiffened, this time in the best of ways, and then he yielded to me entirely, melting into me, our tongues battling for position. Desire ignited in me. I wanted him. All of him.

My fingers found the waistband of his yoga pants. Just as they slid in, my head jerked sideways as he shoved it away from him. His hand landed on the tree next to me, his chest rising and falling, his other hand still clutching my back.

I took advantage of his weakness, sliding around him.

His hand ripped from my back and landed squarely on my chest, creating distance between us.

"No," he panted.

Tingles immediately ran through my body and not because of his fingers gripping my chest. Crap. The rules of consent applied to everything, and the gods and goddesses ensured that, while on campus, the rule would be adhered to. A wavering magickal wall formed between us, and only Jace could break it.

He nodded stiffly at me, spun around, and stomped away. I fell back against the tree, trailing my fingers along the rough bark, trying to figure out what the fuck had just happened, and why it had to end.

CHAPTER
SIXTEEN

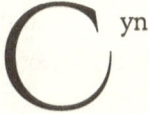yn

CANYON and I never found his mother. He gave me a tour of the campus, though. I'd only seen a small part of it before the Induction Ceremony, and all my classes had been in the main building today. Well, technically Weapons Training had been outside, but we'd entered by way of a doorway in the dungeons. Canyon pointed out the expansive Wildwood Preserves, the stables, and dozens of other locations on campus. I couldn't wait to explore all the trails he told me about.

Plus, I got to see the main building of Silverwood Academy from the outside. It was a gorgeous stone castle complete with turrets and towers but shaped like a star. I'd never seen anything like it. Foreboding and inviting at the same time.

We talked for hours about anything and everything as

we wound our way around the campus. He even shared his mom's tragic vampire story with me. A cruel twist of fate had brought that life to her. After giving birth to him, she kept losing blood. In a last-ditch effort save her, the doctors gave her a blood transfusion, but she was too far gone to survive. Surprise, surprise, when she woke up in the morgue with a hankering for blood. A worker found her emptying blood bags, then she drained him too. Apparently, some of the blood during the transfusion was tainted with vampire blood, which is known for its healing properties, but she'd been too far depleted for it to help her human life. It was enough to turn her into a vampire. The trail of bodies at the hospital and the surrounding area brought the Elitests, who I guess are like the supernatural police force or something. They sent her to Silverwood Prison for six months.

Six months! I thought twenty-one days was too freaking long. But after putting her time in and gaining control over her bloodlust, the Academy invited her to join their teaching staff since she had been a professor of paranormal activities at a prestigious university. After Canyon graduated from the local high school, he was permitted to attend Silverwood Academy, and that's how we wound up at my bedroom door.

"I had a great time tonight," he murmured, staring down at me. I looked up at him, lost in his dreamy eyes.

"Me too." Nerves tangled inside of me but also something else. Something primal. I wanted him to kiss me.

He stood there a long time as if contemplating his next course of action. Finally, he leaned down and kissed my forehead.

"Sleep well, Cynda. I'll see you tomorrow."

"Okay," I whispered, afraid my voice would betray me,

as I watched him disappear down the hall. For the first time since this bizarre new world began, the prospect of possibility flickered inside me. I had assumed romance was dead. After all, who would want to date someone who could drain the lifeblood right out of them?

Canyon, evidently, and I didn't need to compel him this time. He had chosen to give me a tour and talk to me of his own free will.

I slipped into my room, smiling to myself.

"What in the hells are you so happy about?" Dez asked from her bed.

I sighed. Couldn't I just get a second to enjoy the past couple hours without my sister interfering?

"Spill," she ordered, appearing in front of me and invading my space without allowing an exit.

"Back off," I snarled, tired of getting pushed around. I didn't care if she was older or more familiar with this life. She wasn't the only predator in the room.

"Fair enough."

She watched me as she gave me some breathing room. I slipped around her and slumped on my bed.

"Where were you?" she asked.

"Out."

"Descriptive. Out with whom?"

My sister's tenacious nature might kill me. Again. If I didn't feed her something, she'd keep at me.

"Canyon," I said, careful not to add any emotion into it.

"All this time?"

I groaned, throwing my hand over my eyes. "Yes. We went for a walk. He gave me a tour of the grounds and the buildings. That was it."

"You don't need to justify your actions to me. He was delicious, by the way."

I sprang up. "You didn't."

Her purple eyes glinted with mischief. "Too easy. I didn't touch him. All I meant was that he's good looking. Lighten up. It's not even fun to mess with you."

She returned to playing with a strand of beads.

"What are those?"

Her hands stilled. "These? Just pagan prayer beads. Jace gave them to me."

My turn to dig into her closet. "Who's Jace?"

"Hunky is my Meditation and Yoga instructor. He, too, is a delicious piece of manflesh."

I gasped. "You can't date a professor."

Her eyes narrowed at me. "Why not?"

"Because there are rules."

Dez shook her head. "No, no, no. High school? Yes, gross. Pedophiles, no thank you. But in college . . . Hells, we're not even in college. We're at Silverwood Academy, training for the Sisterhood. Besides, we're two consenting adults. Well, I was consenting." She sat up and spun to face me. "Did you know that when consent is revoked, a magickal wall separates you?"

I did not know that. "Did he put you in an uncomfortable situation and then realize he overstepped?"

Her fingers skimmed up and down the beads in their own sort of dance. "Gods, no. I wanted to take advantage of him. He put the brakes on, pulling the 'No' card."

My eyes widened as another gasp left my mouth.

She gave me her trademark devilish grin. "Living with me means you need to get over your virginal ways. And that reminds me, your schedule will change soon."

"I'm not a virgin," I muttered before realizing the full meaning of her words. "Why? What did you do?"

"Why's it always accusations with you?"

"Because you killed me."

She rolled her eyes. "You're always going to hurl that at my face, aren't you?"

"Yes, but why the schedule change?"

She glanced over each shoulder as if checking to see if anyone was watching us. Paranoid much? She slipped over to my bed and slid next to me. I tilted away from her.

She huffed. "I'm not going to hurt you, Cyn. Trust me."

"Trust has to be earned, and you've a long way to go."

"Regardless," she whispered, "stay away from Professor Goldwell. I don't know why. I can't even tell you how I know, but before your next class, you should have a new one."

My heart fluttered as my mind went to Canyon. Did that mean I couldn't see him again? Hopefully Dez had forgotten they were related.

"And that goes for Canyon too."

My heart broke. He was the one person who made me feel normal. Made me feel human.

"I didn't sign up for this life," I whispered, finally putting into words the thoughts plaguing me.

"We were born into it. Whether you've accepted you'd eventually change into a vampire or not, it's our life now."

"I know."

We sat quietly for a while. It was nice, actually. Just being in the same room without fighting, without arguing, without being on edge, and then Dez had to go and ruin it.

"There's one more thing . . ." she said, leaving it to dangle in the air.

I let it drop, my stomach too in knots to take the bait.

She continued anyway. "According to Jace, it's not common for Lilith, or any of the goddesses for that matter, to hang out with the students much. At all, actually, after the Induction Ceremony."

I tilted my head toward her. "Why?"

"I don't know . . ." She let her thought hang before continuing. "You saw her, right? She talked to both of us together. She ate breakfast with us."

"She did."

She blew air out of her mouth. "I knew I wasn't crazy. Jace seemed so surprised when Lilith showed up to tell off Goldwell tonight, and even more so when I told him we've hung out with her since the Induction Ceremony." She chewed on her lip. She did that when she was thinking about something.

"Can he be trusted?"

She snapped back to the present. "Jace?"

I nodded.

"I think so. There's something about him . . ."

"Other than sexual appeal?"

She moaned. "He drips of it."

"Let's not talk about dripping and sex in the same sentence."

She punched my shoulder. "Get your mind out of the gutter."

I snorted and then clamped my hand over my mouth. I never made that sound in public. It was gross and unlady-like—at least that's what my "mom" had always told me.

"Girl," Dez said. "You gotta let that shit out. Dad snorted all the time, just like that. He said we needed to embrace every side of ourselves, and those who snort, do."

"You."

"What's that?"

"You. He told you. There was no 'we.' I wasn't in the picture."

She spun her body to face me. "Cyn, that's where you're wrong. You were always in the picture. He talked about you all the time. Always said to me, 'Dez, everything I teach you, you must teach to your sister when the time is right.'"

My nose itched as unbidden emotions welled up inside me. "Then why didn't he keep me? Why did he give me away?"

"Because he wanted at least one of us to live a normal life. He chose you."

Her voice reeked of bitterness.

"Why can't we tell people we talk to Lilith? The other initiates ate breakfast with her too."

Dez tilted her head, studying me. Her forehead furrowed. "Did they, though? It was just the three of us at our table."

I forgot about that. "True, but why can't we tell anyone? She selected us."

Her eyes shot to her prayer beads, suddenly too absorbed in them to look at me.

"What is it, Dez?"

She shoved off my bed. "Nothing. It's nothing. Get some sleep. We've got a big day tomorrow."

"Unless you muck up my schedule again."

Her purple eyes shot to mine. "I didn't muck it up. There's something else at play here. I can feel it in my gut."

"That might just be dinner. Perhaps Hunky?"

She winked, returning to herself. "I'll never tell. Your gut is the one full of blood. Canyon's blood to be exact."

At the mention of him, everything that made me a woman tightened.

"Good night, Cyn. Sweet dreams," she said, climbing into her bed. "By the look on your face, I suspect your dreams won't be sweet. More spice, and everything oh-so nice. After all, you were the one who said you weren't a virgin."

I gasped. I had never talked about sex with my friends growing up. Dez hurled sexual innuendos around like it was her day job.

"So easy," she laughed, curling under her blankets.

"Yeah, you are."

Two could play at that game.

SEVENTEEN

D^{ez}

Long after I left Cyn's bed and climbed into mine, I continued playing with the pagan prayer beads Jace gave me. My enhanced vampire vision allowed me to study them in the dark without Cyn's judging eyes. I had to hand it to my sister, though. Her budding sarcastic personality impressed me. I thanked the goddesses for that. No need to worry about her remaining a boring stick-in-the-mud who hid under a rock until someone came to save her. So far, she'd proven that wasn't the case.

I fingered the charms attached to the strand. The owl charm represented Lilith. A bird of the night. Mysterious, ever present, ever watchful. The pentagram charm with the circle around it held special meaning to me. I grew up on tales of Mom and her missions with Silver Dagger Sisterhood, and Dad's with Silver Cloak Brotherhood. Mom had worked solo most of the time. Her last mission had taken her into the Underworld to stop a demon shifter from raising Lucifer by using Maleficium—real bad magick. Contrary to popular belief, Lucifer wasn't inherently evil, but if any being is summoned with ill intentions, it tended to mess up the true nature of the individual until the evil could be exorcised. Try exorcising Lucifer. Better to stop it from happening in the first place, which she did. But immediately after that was when she went to the hospital with early labor pains. Cyn was born, Mom disappeared, and the rest was history.

Dad had kept the memories of Mom alive in me, but Cyn never got the chance to know her or hear her stories. I fingered the prayer beads. Each spoke to me in a different way, some stronger than others. My index finger and thumb ran over the irregularly shaped red jasper beads. The gems called to me, and not because the color reminded me of blood or the pulse of Jace's neck, but in a deeper, more fundamental manner.

My fingers traced over the azurite and moonstone beads. Cyn's question about whether Jace could be trusted came back to me. I felt he could be. His explanation of how each crystal represented Lilith rang true with me. I didn't pretend to be an expert geologist or gemologist or crystal hoarder, but I knew enough to listen when they spoke to me. Someone who worked in the fine arts of metal and beadwork spent a lot of time in their own head, contemplating, thinking, manifesting . . . I trusted Jace, but there was something he wasn't telling me, and I planned to find out what.

Lilith's crystals warmed in my hand as if agreeing with me. Why couldn't Cyn and I tell anyone about our meetings with Lilith? Half of Silverwood Academy was dedicated to the goddesses. Did Jace expect me to believe that the other goddesses didn't visit their initiates? But those gold eyes had burned with sincerity when he asked me not to share that information . . .

What was he anyway? Of course, it didn't matter. Rules of attraction applied to all walks of life, but that didn't mean I wasn't curious. I didn't think he was a vampire. He didn't smell sweet, but his musk scent was seductive as hell. He drew me to him by his mere existence.

I finally fell asleep, fantasizing about the way his body felt pressed against mine and the taste of his tongue penetrating my mouth. Yes, my dreams definitely weren't going to be sweet tonight. They rarely were.

CYN HOVERED BESIDE MY HEAD, shaking my shoulders, growling, "Get up. Get up."

I peeked an eyelid open. This cruel and unusual punishment would be her last if she wanted to live.

"Turn the lights off."

"The lights aren't on. It's called sunlight. That's what happens when the sun comes up and shines into a room."

Any warm and fuzzy feelings I might have felt toward my sister last night were gone now in the light of day. Contrary to popular belief, vampires can go out in sunlight. The old wives' tales that vampires turned to ash was just a way to make people feel brave and not completely vulnerable to vamps, at least during daylight hours. The truth was, newly turned vamps' eyes were hypersensitive to bright light, so if you met a vamp wearing sunglasses, chances are they might drain you.

"It can't be morning," I whined. "I just went to bed."

"What you want and the truth are two different things. It's not my fault you didn't sleep last night. Besides, it sounded like you were sleeping to me. Gasps, moans, and I —" she cut off, her face blushing.

"What?"

"Were you having a sex dream about Jace?" she shrieked.

I grinned, closing my eyes. "Yes, I had several dreams starring Hunky. Some with him on top. Some with me. It was a very busy and exhausting night."

"Whatever. I don't want to know. Do we have to share a room? Maybe we can get separate ones."

I slid out of bed and stretched. "You don't want to room with me?"

"If you're that loud in your dreams, I don't want to be in the same room when you're actually having sex."

I yanked off my tank from yesterday and put a fresh one on. I ran my hands over my chest and down my waist, then rested them on my hips. I might not have had sex for real, but I definitely felt sated. My fingers had worked magick last night. I sighed, stretching from side to side. I even touched my toes. Had to keep limber for future sexcapades with Jace. Preferably real ones. Contrary to his actions last night, it was only a matter of time before we slipped between the sheets, or against a tree, this time without clothes on.

I stretched again, arching my back. "So, what's my schedule for today, Little Sister?"

Cyn seemed to like keeping track of mundane things, so I figured she could do that for me. Give her purpose and all that. I didn't have Meditation again until tomorrow, but I needed to talk with Jace about things that had nothing to do with sex. Well, not at first anyway. Who knew where our rendezvous would go after that?

"This morning we have Riding together."

"Is that seriously a class? Are we really going to have to ride horses? Because there are definitely other things I'd prefer to ride."

She groaned and followed me out into the hall. "I really don't need to hear about you and your nocturnal sexual ramblings.

"Vampires," a voice hissed.

I immediately went on edge. My female bits might have been satisfied, but I was always ready for a fight. "Got a problem?"

I eyed a short female I recognized from one of my classes yesterday. Silvery-purple hair. Cross smile. Definitely a pixie with an attitude. My least favorite type.

"Maybe I have a problem with you," she snarled.

Oh, this would be fun. I strolled over to her. She didn't back away. She didn't even blink. It was kinda freaky, to be honest, and I admired her ballsiness, though it was completely idiotic given the number of ways I could disable her.

"It normally takes someone at least a week before they realize they don't like me."

"A week? Try a day," Cyn murmured behind me.

"I was trying to be nice, but my sister's right. Usually people hate me by the end of the day."

She clapped. "Well, point for you. I hated you the second I first laid eyes on you."

I gestured to my eyes. "It's the purple, isn't it? You wish that your eyes were the same shade of purple to match your hair."

She gasped. "That's not it. I hate vampires, period."

"That's awfully discriminatory, Azalea." A redhead strolled between us, breaking our line of sight. "Hey, Cyn. This your sister, Dez?"

I recognized the redhead from the other night. She had been the first to take the challenge. Magickal energy pooled around her. A witch if I ever saw one. "Brigit, right?"

"Yes, Brigit selected me. I'm Anastasia." She stuck out her hand.

I stared at it hovering in the air, waiting for me to shake it, for one, two, three seconds until she pulled it back.

"Okay . . . so you're not a handshaker. Cyn calls me Red."

"My sister is very original."

She laughed. I instantly liked her based on her reaction alone, and I normally didn't like people period.

Cyn looked from me to Red and back to me. "I thought once we got into the Academy, we'd all get along. Everyone being Sisterhood hopefuls and all that."

I shook my head. "Oh, how young and naive you are."

"I have to agree with your sister, Cyn. Each of us might be a supernatural, blessed by a goddess, even gifted in one or more of the elements, but the bottom line is, we are women. And though some of us," Anastasia, a.k.a. Red, gestured at Cyn, me, and herself, "embrace our feminine side and seek to foster long-lasting friendships with other women, there are others who see other women as competition in the classroom, in love, in life. They'd rather compete against one another than pick each other up."

The skin on Cyn's forehead bunched together. "Why would they do that? We aren't in a competition here. We're in the Sisterhood."

I wagged my finger at her. "Not yet, we aren't. We're at

the Academy and not all of us will get invited into the Sisterhood."

"The best of us will," snarled Azalea, overhearing at least part of our conversation.

Red stepped toward her. "Azalea, why do you keep showing up, and why do you always have to pick a fight?"

"Why shouldn't I?" she cried, backpedaling away from Red. She seemed more wary of Red's witch powers than my vampire abilities. Interesting . . .

Red flung her hand out as she spun back toward us. Azalea fell flat on her ass. Red's green eyes sparkled in amusement as she looped her arms through each of ours and paraded us down the hall. Surprisingly, I let her take mine without throat-punching her.

"That's a violation of school rules," Azalea shrieked.

Red glanced over her shoulder. "I don't know what you're talking about. I've got two witnesses to your . . ." her head swung side to side as if searching for someone, ". . . none. You have no one to corroborate your story."

Azalea shot her hand at Cyn, then me. "You both saw it."

"I don't know what you're talking about. Looked to me like you tripped over an air pocket or something, and Red doesn't control Air." Of course, Cyn and I did, but I wasn't about to remind the little twit.

"Plus, we're vampires," Cyn added. "You said we can't be trusted, so . . ."

I beamed at her. She made me proud to call her sister. Red rehooked our arms, and we twirled back around, heading to the cafeteria.

"I really like you, Dez. My vision was correct."

I nodded. I'd spent my life on the road with Dad, so I'd met plenty of seers in my time. Unfortunately, none of them foresaw his death. Or else they hadn't bothered to mention it to me or him.

"I thought that was a secret between us," Cyn whispered.

Red tightened her hold on our arms, drawing us to her. "It is. Between the three of us. I trust Dez too."

"You're the only one," Cyn said under her breath.

"Love you too, Sis. Love you too."

CHAPTER
EIGHTEEN

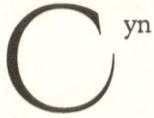yn

Sometimes my sister and I really clicked, like the way we combined forces with Red when Azalea tried bullying us. Then other times, like at breakfast when she burped loud enough for half the people eating to hear her, then proceeded to announce she was full and had to take a . . . well, you can guess. Those times I couldn't see the family resemblance if I tried. I kept things locked up tight. My personal business was my personal business. My inner demons were my inner demons, but Dez tossed hers around for all the world and could give two shits to the wind what everyone else thought about them. (Her words not mine.)

And if I was being honest, her friendship with Red bummed me out. When Anastasia said we'd become great friends, I had assumed it was just with me. But now Dez was a part of that lifelong friendship too. I wanted one thing that was just mine in this new world, but Red wasn't it.

"What's bugging you?"

I glanced over at my sister, her light purple eyes watching me. There was no denying we shared at least part of a family tree. I had ignored that similarity before, but after staring at my light green eyes in the mirror, I saw the purple strands in them, just like hers, and evidently, just like the actual fluorite crystal. Canyon had promised to give me one as soon as he found the "right" one—whatever that meant—but I'd keep that to myself since I was supposed to stay away from him.

I planned to talk to him today and fish around for the reason his mom was dangerous. I mean, the Academy had hired her to work here. How terrible could she be? Besides, what Dez didn't know wouldn't hurt her.

She waved her hand in front of my face. "Hellooo, anybody home?"

I blinked. "Sorry, lost in thought."

"It happens," Red said. "I do it all the time, but then, I spent a lot of my childhood by myself with only my pets and my mom to keep me company. Luckily, I've got you two now!"

"Whether we like it or not," Dez chuckled.

Red laughed along with her. "Oh, you definitely like it."

I couldn't imagine friendly, outgoing Anastasia growing up without anyone to talk to. I wanted to find out her backstory, but it was too early in our relationship. I didn't want to make it weird or awkward between us. I was weird and awkward enough without adding to it.

"I can't believe the three of us have this class together."

"What's with a riding class? I don't even get it."

"I can't wait," Red exclaimed.

"Let me guess. You watched *Brave* when you were little and pictured yourself as a young princess Merida riding her beloved steed across the countryside, shooting arrows out of your arse."

"How do you know that Merida wasn't based on my own childhood?"

Dez's jaw dropped.

Red giggled. "So easy."

I laughed along with her. Red had bested Dez in her own game. Wonder how she liked it.

We followed the stone path down the winding hill to the barn. Herds of horses grazed in the fields around us as we made our way to the riding ring where a small group of students waited for class to begin.

Despite Anastasia's magick, my butt muscles were still sore from training with Professor Bladecroft yesterday. She had worked my gluteus maximus to the max, and the prospect of riding today pained muscles I didn't know I had. But with all those beautiful horses, it'd be worth it.

It had been a few years since I rode, but it really was like riding a bike.

A few horses neighed to us as we joined the other students. I wandered over and let them sniff my hand before rubbing an Appaloosa under her chin. A bay pranced over and tried shoving the app out of the way.

"Now, now, I've got two hands and can scratch both of you."

That seemed to satisfy him. Red joined me and took over tending to the bay. A palomino soon searched for attention too. More and more horses appeared, seeking scratches or treats.

"Come on, Dez," I called over my shoulder. "Say hello to our instructors."

"Our instructors," she grumbled. "Pains in the asses, if you ask me."

"Tell us what you really think," a woman behind us said.

Red and I, along with the rest of the class, turned to face a tall woman with intricate braids trailing down the sides of her face and back. She wore tan britches and a white collared shirt with the Academy's emblem on it, along with tall black riding boots.

"So, we're riding English?" I asked, excitement rising within me.

She tapped a whip in her palm as she watched me. "And what makes you say that?"

I regretted speaking aloud without raising my hand. My cheeks reddened.

"No need to worry about calling out. I like enthusiastic students, so long as they're not overly excited once on their horse."

The need to defend myself and prove my worth pushed aside my earlier embarrassment. "No, definitely not."

"Excellent, so explain to everyone why you assumed we were riding English today." Her warm brown eyes filled me with courage.

I licked my lips. "Sure, well, your britches are a trademark of English riding, along with the collared shirt, creating a polished, finished look, but also your tall riding boots and whip. They're English riding equipment."

"As opposed to . . ." Dez said. Apparently we shared another family trait: calling out instead of raising our hand.

My eyes met the professor's.

"Go ahead."

"Well, if we were riding Western, she'd wear maybe jeans, a button-down shirt, and cowgirl boots. Of course, the easiest way to figure it out would be the saddle. The Western saddle has a horn, a wider padded seat, more leather, maybe silver bling, leather fenders, and bulky stirrups that hang down. It weighs a lot and is placed on a thick wool blanket saddle pad. The rider uses weight and neck reining to ride as opposed to the close contact of an English saddle. An English saddle is smooth leather, no horn, the leather straps and stirrups are tucked up near the saddle until ready to ride, and it's a lot lighter than a Western saddle."

"Excellent explanation. Though I expect much of it went over your classmates' heads, at least on their first day. Is it safe to assume you've ridden?"

"Yes, I owned two horses. I first rode Western Pleasure when I was younger, then switched to English for the challenge and excitement. Western Pleasure got boring aside from the bling. Too slow."

The professor's lips curved up as if in agreement.

"I switched to hunter jumper, started learning dressage, and then . . ." I swallowed, not expecting the rush of emotions to surge up. "Well, life took an unexpected turn."

She nodded. "As it does sometimes. Not to worry, though. You will assist me during class, and we'll discuss more riding opportunities after."

A rush of excitement surged through me. I couldn't wait. My dad had lost his job with his old law firm, and we'd had to sell the horses. It was the hardest day of my life, saying goodbye to Rainy and Sunny.

"My name is Tiana Lippincott."

Murmurs rose up around us. Since I hadn't grown up in the supernatural world, I must have missed out on her notoriety.

"You can call me Professor Tiana or Professor T." She

clasped her hands behind her back and paced in front of us. "So, Riding 101. We will begin with horses."

"Begin with, as in we will be riding things besides horses?" Dez asked, hopeful to get out of riding horses as quickly as possible.

A male voice behind me purred just loud enough for me and a few others to hear. "I can think of something else you can ride bareback, like all night long."

Dez spun around, kicking her leg out. I followed the movement as her extended leg hit his stomach, causing him to land on his ass. She narrowed her eyes at him, dropping into a lunge with her fists raised. "Ever hear of sexual harassment? I warned you yesterday there would be consequences."

The very muscular guy pushed himself off the ground and prowled toward Dez, who didn't seem the least bit intimidated, though he towered over her. Professor Tiana appeared between them, throwing her hands up. "Deziree, this boy harassed you before?"

Dez scowled at him. "Yes."

"It wasn't sexual harassment. Ever hear of a joke? An innuendo?"

Professor Tiana threw up her hand, instantly silencing him. "You will be revisiting Silverwood Prison to get your primal mouth under control, and if you can't, permanent consequences will be given."

"I didn't—"

"Enough. Now, either I can have someone escort you, or you can admit yourself."

"But—"

"Do not make me reevaluate my decision, because the outcome will not be as favorable."

He dropped his gaze to the ground. "Yes, ma'am. I'll go

myself."

"Best get to it then," Dez snapped.

He pursed his lips but kept his head down as he backed away.

Professor Tiana double-clapped her hands loudly. "Alrighty then. Now, who wants to meet their first mount?"

Every hand shot up, including my sister's. She claimed she didn't get along with horses, but Professor Tiana had proved she was no pushover, immediately earning Dez's respect.

My mind reeled following the incident. My time at Silverwood Prison was dark and unpleasant. I never even considered the possibility that we could actually get sent back there if we broke the rules. Of course, the threat was there, but I assumed it was just that, a threat. A chill ran down my spine at the possibility. I could never lose myself in bloodlust again. Not if I wanted to live. Because, if I had to return to Silverwood Prison, I wouldn't go willingly.

Professor T stopped at the first stall. A head popped out, but it didn't belong to a horse.

"We ride dragons?" Red exclaimed.

Professor T smiled. "We do, but this one is still a baby. That's why it's in the stall. We won't get to dragon riding until later in the semester." She strolled to the next stall, and a giant bird head appeared, snapping its powerful beak. Professor T scratched its feathered head and murmured a few words to it. It closed its mouth, pushing its head into her hand for more attention.

I peeked inside the stall. Giant wings sprung out from its sides. I glanced down and saw taloned toes. Black eyes blinked, watching me.

"We ride griffins?" a guy behind me asked.

"Some will. It depends on if they like you and if they

allow you to ride them. Griffins are very particular about who rides them. Grousie was injured during her most recent flight and is on stall rest while she recovers."

Red raised her hand. "Grousie? As in the bird?"

"Exactly like the bird. Grousie enjoys the irony of the name, don't you?" she murmured to the griffin in a very sweet voice. Grousie purred like a cat. I blinked, unable to believe my eyes. During my short time as a Sempiternal, I'd gotten somewhat used to hanging around other supernaturals, but supernatural creatures took it to a whole other level of awesomeness.

"Wow," I whispered. Several classmates concurred with my sentiment.

"Wow, is right. Isn't it, Grousie?"

Grousie shook its head in agreement.

"It can understand you?" a guy behind me asked.

Grousie's head tilted as if it did understand what we were saying.

"They are highly intelligent but very sensitive. They get offended easily.

"Sounds like my last boyfriend," Red whispered.

Dez snickered but kept it quiet so as not to upset the griffin.

Dez walked with Professor T as they continued down the barn aisle. "First, do you have any fire-breathing unicorns? Because I won't go near one of them without a weapon."

"I don't blame you, and we do not."

"Any pegasus? I've always wanted one of those."

I caught up to them. "Aren't those a tad too horse-like for you?"

"Well, sure, but they can fly. That's every girl's fantasy."

"Not every girl's," I said.

"Oh, sorry. I forgot, Miss I-Had-Two-Horses," she sneered in a snotty voice.

"Are you pretending to be me? Because it sounds like you've got a stick up your butt."

"You're the one with the stick up it," she growled, flashing her canines at me.

"Is that supposed to scare me? 'Cause I've got them too." My fangs elongated, and I curled my lips back, revealing them to her.

"Ladies, chill." Anastasia rested her hands on each of us, instantly relaxing me. She regularly broke one of the Academy's rules, but no one, especially not me or Dez, would sell her out. Once our fangs retracted and our shoulders softened, she patted us again like we were her favorite pets. "That's better. Now, I don't know about you, but I can't wait to meet my majestic mount."

Dez stopped at one of the open stall doors, and there sat a shiny chrome-plated Harley Davidson. "We get to ride motorcycles too?"

"And Mustangs. Ever wonder where the term horsepower came from?" Professor T called to us. She stood at the far end of the rear paddock, but apparently she could still hear us, so she had probably heard us fighting. A sister squabble better not get us tossed back into Silverwood Prison, because if so, we'd wind up having permanent residence.

"You had me at Mustang," Dez shouted as she ran outside. I slowly walked behind her. Her full black curls bounced around as she joined Professor T. I needed to find out what actions could send someone back to Silverwood Prison, because my sister tested my patience, and I'm not gonna lie. Sometimes I wanted to drive a stake through her heart.

NINETEEN

ez

I'D NEVER ADMIT it to my sister, but Riding class was amazing. Long before the fire-breathing unicorn incident, horses and I had never gotten along, but that might have been because I was a tad too aggressive with them. I know that's hard to believe, but it's true.

During a mission involving a fallen angel, Dad and I took up temporary residence at a trailer across the street from a horse farm. It wasn't easy making friends—probably because I was a tad too aggressive with them too—but also because we moved a lot, and after a few sad goodbyes, I'd stopped trying to make new ones. I usually made animal friends with no problem, though. And that's why I had sprinted across the street, jumped the fence, and raced up to the herd with my arms fanned wide. They scattered. Well, all except for the stallion, who didn't appreciate my enthusiasm and chased me across the field, through the fence, and most likely would have followed me into the trailer if I hadn't slammed the door on him. I stayed away from the herd after that, especially since, whenever I left the trailer, that ornery stallion stomped its hoof in warning.

Thankfully, Dad took care of the fallen angel quickly, and we were onto the next mission.

But today, after Professor T explained the proper way to approach a horse, I cautiously extended my hand to a cute palomino paint who sniffed it and allowed me to scratch her face. Soon after, she decided we were besties and allowed me to tack her up and ride her without complaint. No buck. No kick in the ass. Just the perfect ride. A win in my book.

The afternoon, however, had proven to be an epic fail thus far because I couldn't find Jace anywhere. Either he was avoiding me or he wasn't on campus, and I had questions. A lot of questions.

But just as I was leaving the hallway where the meditation studio was, a deep baritone voice called out, "Hey."

My insides tightened in the best of ways. Was it possible to orgasm by just hearing someone talk? I couldn't wait to find out.

I slowly spun around to face him. I didn't want to seem too anxious or anything. Make Hunky want me as much as I wanted him.

I studied my nails to appear disinterested. "Hi. Fancy meeting you here."

"Since you've passed my bedroom doorway three times this afternoon, I'd say our meeting isn't a surprise at all."

Busted. Time to distract. "You sleep in your meditation studio?"

He grinned. "My sleeping quarters are attached to it. Just like they are for every professor."

"Huh. I didn't know that."

He winked. "Now you do."

His very presence left my knees shaky. I feigned confidence. It's how I'd survived much deadlier encounters than this. I strolled toward him. "Funny you should know that I've walked by here already. Were you watching me?"

He tapped his head. "I have my ways."

Not sure what he meant by that, but I wasn't about to let him know that.

"I bet." I placed my finger on his chest as I licked my lips. Heat radiated between us. "Why is it you called it your bedroom when this door enters your studio? Is getting me in your bed the first thing that comes to mind?"

He blinked, then cleared his throat. "Deziree, is there something you'd like?"

I winked. "A whole lot of somethings. But first, I've got a few questions."

He leaned toward me right where I wanted him. "Questions?"

"Yes."

I withdrew the pagan prayer bead strand he'd given me the day before. His eyes fell on it, and he immediately relaxed.

"What is it you'd like to know?"

I tilted my head toward the door. "Should we go in?"

"Uh . . ." He took a deep breath, his nostrils flaring in and out as if trying to catch my scent. Again I wondered what he was. I couldn't place his earthy smell, but I was willing to explore his mouth and body to find out. He cleared his throat. "Let's go outside."

I took off down the hall toward the exit we'd used the

night before. "If you say so, but remember what happened out there."

He groaned as if he did in fact remember what had happened out there. The sound did things to me that ought to be illegal, at least in public, but again, I wasn't about to let him know that.

I approached our tree, but instead of leaning against it, I folded down under it into a seated position. With its giant overhanging branches, the tree offered privacy that would come in handy later, but I wanted to question him first.

He sat down across from me and pointed at the prayer beads. "Do you have questions about that?"

"I do. You mentioned it represented Lilith but that some of the crystals weren't commonly used on behalf of the goddess."

"I did," he said slowly.

"I was brought up living and breathing a supernatural hunter's life. Did you know that?"

He ran his hands down his thighs, curling them over his knees. "I did not. Your parents?"

"Dad, actually. My mom disappeared after Cyn's birth, most likely dead."

"But you two didn't grow up together."

Interesting that he knew that . . .

"No, my dad gave her away. She's new to this life. Didn't even know it existed. Not until I drove her car into a tree."

"You forced the Change."

"I did. By killing her, did she become a turned vampire instead of a born one?"

He tilted his head, his gold eyes watching me. "Why are you asking me and not one of your other professors? You know I only recently graduated."

"But you *are* in the Brotherhood."

He breathed in and out. "I am."

"My dad was in the Brotherhood too, and I was worried that someone older and who worked here longer might try to hide certain truths from me."

I had intended to ask Alexander Logan yesterday after class, but he wouldn't even speculate about Cyn's potential abilities until he tested her over the next few weeks. He also flat-out refused to tell me why my own abilities only resurfaced after his elemental attack in class. I doubted he'd answer my simple question.

His gold eyes brightened as if boring into my brain and discovering the truth, but still wanting me to say it anyway. "But you don't think I would?"

My fingers trailed up and down the beads. "No. You warned me last night to stay away from . . ." I looked around the courtyard to make sure we were alone but decided to mouth the words anyway, ". . . you know who."

He grinned, silently saying, "I do, and I did."

I pursed my lips, breathing in and out. Everything we had talked about was imprinted in my brain. Even his touch. His smell. They had to be imprinted in his too.

"So, is she turned or born?"

He ran his fingers through his hair. Mine twitched to join them in those sexy locks. He closed his eyes as if concentrating on my question and searching for an answer. Finally, he opened them.

"I don't know. It's too early to tell."

Not the answer I wanted to hear. "When?"

He shrugged.

"When there's a line of dead bodies pointing to her?"

"You know even with turned vampires that's not always

the case. Emotions and past history play a vital role in determining future actions."

"She was a sheltered goody-two-shoes who wanted to go into the sciences before I killed her."

"She would have changed eventually."

"I know, but she doesn't completely believe that yet."

"She will. She'll know that you only had her best interests in mind when you took matters into your own hands."

Not entirely true, but I'd go along with it. I jerked my chin up and down, my nose itching with unwanted emotion.

He leaned toward me and wrapped his hands around my head, drawing me to him. I smiled to myself. I liked a man who knew what he wanted. But instead of kissing me, he tilted my head and whispered in my ear. "You probably saved her life by turning her early. She's safe here."

My forehead bunched. If she was safe here, it meant she was in danger out in the world. Were those Children of the Sun who chased us the night I abducted her after me, or her, or worse—both of us?

But my thoughts became clouded the longer Jace remained near me, overloading all my senses. My hormones wanted to take control and climb into his lap and have my way with him. His nose dipped to my neck, inhaling deeply before he broke away and returned to his cross-legged seated position across from me.

As my senses returned, I took a deep breath to further clear my mind. "I have more questions."

A delicious dimple popped in on his cheek. "I suspect you do, but the time and place is not now."

I licked my lips, gathering my thoughts. His eyes tracked the movement, which nearly derailed me, but my need for answers overrode my horniness. Well, for now, anyway.

"Is Adam the counterpart to Lilith?"

His eyes widened as he blinked a few times. Definitely not the question he was expecting. "No. No, he isn't. Both Adam and Lilith were made from the same clay by Mother Earth and Father Sky. Adam tried to dominate Lilith in every manner a woman can be dominated. He raped her. Wanted her to serve him. Belittled her. She left, refusing to be subservient to him. Adam failed the experiment, but neither Mother Earth nor Father Sky had it in them to take his life. That's when the dawn of Christianity bloomed, and Lilith's story became twisted into lies and misdeeds. The corruptness of male dominance grew and went so far as making Eve from Adam's rib to serve as his subject rather than his equal. Aside from that, Lilith would never allow Adam to be represented at Silverwood Academy, let alone Silver Cloak Brotherhood. Mother Earth and Father Sky would never allow it either, nor would any of the goddesses or gods. Adam's story grew because, for some, it was easier to swallow. It fed egos and the thirst for power. Boosted false confidence. A real man," he lifted his chest, raising his chin, "doesn't need to dominate women. We are all equals. All children of Mother Earth and Father Sky."

"So, who is Lilith's counterpart then?"

His cheek rose in a crooked grin. "I guess that's why you need to attend class this evening. You'll learn about all the goddesses and gods."

"But you've already told me part of Lilith's story."

"I did because you asked if Adam was her male counterpart. That is an insult to all men."

I wrapped the beads in and out of my hands. In a short time, it had already become a habit.

"One more question."

"Only one?" His eyes sparked with amusement.

"Well, one more for now. Why did you give this to me?" I held the strand up, letting it hang from my hand.

His gaze fell to his knees. "I make them."

Again I sensed he wasn't telling me everything. I wanted him to take ownership. "You had a large bowlful, but I was the only student you gave one to." The beads warmed in my hand as if I'd stumbled upon the truth. "You made them for me, didn't you?"

He reached for the beads but lightly brushed my hand instead. "No. Coincidence."

I pulled away from him. I wasn't going to make this easy for him. I grew up with supernaturals. I knew there was no such thing as coincidence. "Liar."

He looked at me. "It's true."

I pushed myself off the ground, my lips dipping dangerously close to his as I stood up. He swallowed, staring at them as he stood up alongside me. A wisp of air existed between us.

"Well, I ought to be going." I rested my hand on my hip.

He blinked, suddenly aware he was blocking my exit, and stepped out of my path.

I sauntered away, swinging my hips to give him something to fantasize about.

"I'll see you around," I called over my shoulder without looking at him, knowing he couldn't take his eyes off me.

CHAPTER
TWENTY

yn

RIDING class felt like I was taking a step back into my pre–familial-financial-crisis life, when all I had to do was take care of my horses and I could ride whenever I wanted. But life had taken an unexpected turn or two or three. Truthfully, even before my parents—well, my adoptive parents—had sold my horses, my relationship with them had begun deteriorating. Looking back, it was as if they knew I was different, and while they adored their baby girl, the teenage version didn't quite live up to their expectations. Their lack of interest, or maybe should I say disappointment in me, drove me to get the best grades in all my classes. To be the best in every activity I participated in. But still it wasn't enough. Honestly, even my classmates began to distance themselves from me as we entered the last years of high school. If Derrick hadn't guilted me into sleeping with him, even he would have left. I'd spent the last two years of school scrutinizing every pore, every eyelash, every aspect of my face, body, and hair to see if perhaps I'd missed something, wondering whether, if I could alter or change it, all would be forgiven and my friends would come running back. It never happened.

Not when I dyed my hair blond to hide the dark auburn that grew more lush and vibrant with each passing year.

Not when I stopped participating in class, hoping that maybe if I didn't act like such an overachiever, they'd like me again.

Not even when I broke my ankle and my school bag wobbled awkwardly from my arms as I hobbled from class to class. Derrick never even helped with my bag unless I gave him a hand job in the girls' bathroom each morning.

Maybe they sensed the predator emerging in me. That had to be it, but it didn't make it hurt any less.

Now, everyone seemed to like me, aside from Azalea. Anastasia loved me. She loved Dez too, which admittedly I was still jealous about, but given my past history, who could blame me?

Even Canyon, who I was supposed to stay away from, always appeared whenever I wasn't sure where my next class was. He would offer to carry half of the giant stack of books I checked out of the library without even the promise of sex. It made me want him more.

This afternoon, my Meditation and Yoga instructor, Dez's Jace, encouraged us to embrace our insecurities, and I was really trying to. I smiled to myself. I'd never admit it to my sister, but so far as a Sempiternal, so good—as long as I kept my cool around my sister.

Our bedroom door swung open, and Speak-of-the-

Temptress waltzed in. Her behavior immediately put me on edge.

"What are you so happy about?"

She winked at me. "A lady never divulges her secrets." She hopped up on the bed next to me. "Luckily I'm not one of those. I spent time late this afternoon with Hunky and left him wanting me more."

"Did you sleep with Jace? Your . . . our professor?"

She pulled away from me on the bed. "Judgey. He's only a few years older than me, a recent graduate of Silverwood Academy, and thereby doesn't count as a professor."

"Does he teach a class?"

She rolled her eyes. "If that's what you want to call it, I guess."

"Then he's a professor."

She threw up her hands. "Semantics, but whatever. How did your classes go today?"

I narrowed my eyes at her. "Do you mean before or after you embarrassed me in Riding?"

It wasn't the first time I wished that one of the side effects of becoming a bloodsucker was that I could shoot red lasers out of my eyeballs.

Dez pulled back her shoulders. "You're looking at me as if I'm a monster."

"Well, aren't you?"

"I'm no monster. Neither are you. Monsters are the ones who hunt us. Who stake us. Who wrap silver around our wrists and necks. Who want to drain us of the very thing that makes us immortal."

I recognized her diversion tactic, but I wasn't about to be derailed. "Did you have to compare riding a horse to cowgirl position with a guy? That gave me and everyone else in the class the yuckies."

Her face pinched, and she raised an eyebrow. "The yuckies?"

"Grossed out. Disgusted. Heebie-jeebies."

"I didn't even call it the cowgirl position."

I slammed my open palm against my leg, causing a loud smack to echo through the room. "No, you said something more vulgar."

She snorted before clearing her throat. "I apologized for my behavior later in the class. Sometimes words come out of my mouth before I've thought them all the way through. Sometimes I'm impulsive with my actions too, but I *am* trying to restrain myself, especially after what happened to that asshole when we first got to the stables."

Memories of the douchebag and his sexual harassment came rushing back to me. "Your words and your actions were on point with him."

She sighed. "Yes, they were. It burns me that women are subjected to that kind of behavior, wherever they live. Even a goddess isn't completely safe from it." Her words rang with sadness and the heaviness of being a woman in a world filled with men.

"I was afraid to say something. I'm glad you did," I admitted.

She grinned at me. "After learning about Lilith's raw deal this afternoon, I might have castrated the asshole."

I flipped open the book on my lap and showed her the picture of Lilith from the chapter I'd just read. "She does get a bad rap in Christianity."

"Yes, she does, but she's kick-ass." Her lips lifted into a smile.

I laughed along with her. "Yes, she is."

"Hey, listen," she said, gently squeezing my knee, "we can't talk about our interactions with Lilith. I guess it's not that common, and it could cause potential problems for us if the wrong person hears about it."

"You told me that last night."

She sighed. "I know, but something keeps needling at the back of my head, along with this feeling in my stomach that tells me we need to be careful."

"You mean your intuition?"

She nudged me with her shoulder. "Listen, Miss Smarty Pants, whatever it's called, we need to listen to it. Remember . . . uh, never mind. Ready for dinner?"

She wasn't telling me something, and I didn't need to listen to my instincts to know that. "What is it? Remember what?"

She stood up. "Nothing. I'm freaking starving. If I don't get some food and a pint of blood soon, someone will get hurt."

I followed her to the door. She swung it open, but I grabbed her bicep. "Dez, what is it?"

Red appeared at our doorway. "Everything all right here? Am I breaking up a sister-bonding moment?"

Dez jerked free from my hand. "Nope, not at all. I was just telling Cyn that if I didn't eat soon, someone would die a quick death." She whipped her head around and yelled over her shoulder. "Azalea, do you want it to be you?"

"One wrong move and you'll find your ass back in Silverwood Prison like Gerald," she snarled.

"Gerald? That was Mr. Sexual Harassment's name?"

"He didn't sexually harass you. Besides, aren't you an all-powerful vampire? Can't you handle it?"

A growl erupted deep in my sister's chest. A sound I'd never heard before. Her fangs elongated. Her entire body coiled, ready to strike.

Red placed her hand on her shoulder. "The point is,

Azalea, that no woman should be subjected to unwanted advances or innuendos from any man, and if you don't realize that and embrace that truth, you will never make it into Silver Dagger Sisterhood."

"She won't make it until the end of the day," Dez grunted.

"You don't get to decide that," Azalea snapped.

Red laughed. "No, but I'm thinking you're proving to be difficult to your goddess. How is your ability to master Earth?"

She lifted her chest. "Queen Maeb chose me."

"Each goddess selects those she feels embrace her gifts and virtues, but she also selects those who lack in those areas, in hopes that her selection will someday represent the goddess fully."

"That's not true!" Azalea was practically spitting.

Red smiled. "It actually is. Perhaps you should spend some time this evening reading up on Goddess Maeve."

Azalea narrowed her eyes at us, then stomped down the hall.

"You know, for someone so little, she really makes a lot of noise," Dez said. "Thanks for jumping in. I almost lost my head."

"No kidding," Red laughed. "I thought I'd have to spell you again."

We all stopped. Dez and I looked at each other, our eyes wide. "You didn't?"

"No. Touch can prove just as powerful as a spell."

Envy ravaged my insides. Fear too, because I didn't feel anywhere near as powerful or wise as Red on our second day at Silverwood. "How do you know so much about your identity?"

She touched my arm, and tension immediately diffused

147

from my shoulders. "My mom dedicated her life to Brigit. She became a member of the Druid Sisters of the Gallicenial when I left to come here."

Dez turned to her. "Was she in Silver Dagger Sisterhood before that?"

"She was until she had me. She spent her mothering years studying Brigit's ways and learning about the Druid Sisters, and now that I'm gone, she went for it. So, yeah, I know a lot about Brigit, along with the other goddesses, but there is always more to learn."

"Yes, there is," a soft voice barely above a whisper said behind us.

The three of us pivoted in unison like long-time friends.

A tall blond woman stood in the shadows of the hallway. When our eyes fell on her, she rolled her shoulders as if trying to shrink into a rabbit and scurry away. Her whole body shook with fright.

"Hey, we won't hurt you," I murmured, approaching her slowly as if she were a skittish horse.

Her bright blue eyes watched me get closer. She kept blinking, moving her lips, as if she was trying to disappear.

"It's okay. We really won't hurt you." I held out my hand, not because I thought she'd smell it like a horse but maybe so she'd realize she didn't have anything to fear, least of all from me.

The woman tugged on her sleeves, trying to tuck herself inside her shirt. I could just make out the faint blue outline of Water on her top.

"Your goddess is Morrigan, right?"

She nodded.

"She seems really cool."

Cool? Seriously, Cyn? What was this, eighth grade?

Her lips ever so slightly lifted into a grin. "She is cool."

I smiled, careful not to show my teeth. My fangs weren't elongated, but dogs and other pack animals often took the demonstration of teeth as an aggressive act.

Red hung back so as not to crowd us, but Dez crept forward.

"Alyze? I haven't seen you since Demonology. You okay?" Dez said in a calming voice that impressed the heck out of me. I thought she only had one volume: loud and obnoxious.

Alyze's chest rose and fell rapidly. "I've been feeling a little overwhelmed. A lot overwhelmed, actually."

"I get that. The first few days are a lot to take in. Maybe tomorrow afternoon we could find Wildwood Lake and swim. Would you like that?"

Alyze's face lit up. "Really?"

Dez smiled. "Definitely. Hey, this is my sister, Cynda, and that's Anastasia."

"Call me Red," Anastasia offered.

The woman breathed in and out of her nose, visibly relaxing even with our proximity. "I'm Alyze."

"Hi, Alyze. That's a beautiful name, and you can call me Cyn. These two do." I rolled my eyes, acting like the nickname wasn't growing on me as much as it was.

Alyze smiled, her shoulders unrolling, and she stood taller. "Thank you," she whispered.

Red smiled. "Would you like to join us for dinner? We were just heading that way."

She pulled her hand to her chest. "Me?"

"Of course you, Alyze." Red looped her arm in Alyze's like she'd done with Dez and me when we first met her. "I can tell we're going to be fast friends."

Dez hooked Alyze's other arm, which surprised me. Dez wasn't touchy or feely.

"We are?" Alyze asked, her head swinging back and forth between them, but she no longer seemed frightened. Guess sometimes all someone needed to feel comfortable was to feel welcomed.

"I've already seen it," Red added.

I snorted. So much for keeping her seeing abilities a secret. Her green eyes shot to mine.

"Got something to say, Cyn?"

Out of respect, and in case anyone was listening who shouldn't have been, I kept my voice low. "That's three of us you've told so far about your super-secret ability."

She laughed. "True. I told you we were destined to be friends."

"I thought you only meant Cyn and me."

"Nope, Alyze too."

"Anyone else we should know about."

Red stopped, scrunching her nose as if she was in fact seeing the future. "Not yet, but soon."

"I can't wait. I hope it's some delicious pieces of manflesh."

I rolled my eyes. "Of course you do."

Actually, maybe I did too.

CHAPTER
TWENTY-ONE

D^{ez}

THE DAYS FLEW BY. The four of us became inseparable. We helped each other in the classes we were having difficulty in, we ate together, we hung out together. I didn't have one friend growing up, and now I had three, and one of them was my sister.

Twice a week we took Elemental Training together. Of course, Cyn and I had the easiest time with Air, but Water and Fire were fast on their way to becoming our second and third strongest elements, thanks to Alyze and Red. Alyze was a siren, which is why, with her help, even Red began to master Water, despite it being her opposite element. Sirens can also calm the wind with their singing, which explained why she had immediately put me at ease rather than elic-iting my typical bitchiness when I met someone new. You know the stab-first-ask-questions-later motto. Glad I didn't with her or Red, because they were my first girl-friends, and I wanted to keep them.

Jace had come through and changed Cyn's class so she didn't have to attend any lectures with Professor Goldwell. He also kept his distance from me. Whenever I wandered the halls or grounds late at night in hopes of finding him, I'd come home horny and disappointed. Not a good combination. A few of the male students helped scratch that itch —some more competently than others—but they all came up short.

And don't even get me started about Meditation class. Jace would hide on the opposite side of the room and wouldn't even look at me. Whenever I stayed after class to talk, he'd disappear into the hall. And now that I knew his bedroom was just inches from my yoga mat, when I was supposed to be meditating, my concentration had taken a turn for the worse, even with his pagan prayer beads.

I groaned, running my fingers through my hair on the way back to my room after Meditation class.

"Sexually frustrated again?" Alyze asked. She grew more confident every day and was fast becoming a force to be reckoned with. Swimming in Wildwood Lake definitely helped her too.

Attending Silverwood Academy was voluntary, but when she got recruited, her parents had forced her to come. She was most powerful underwater, for obvious reasons, but this was her first time out of the water and, well, familiar with the fish-out-of-water concept? It's true for sirens and mermaids as well. Even mermen. I had one of those the other night, but it still didn't fill what I needed, even when he speared me with his trident.

"I thought you said mermaids do it better," I replied.

"Hands down, they do," Alyze admitted. "I've no idea about mermen, though."

"Trust me, they don't know what to do with their hands or the rest of their accessories."

"Too bad, because you haven't lived until you've slept with a mermaid."

"I like long poky things, but I will take your suggestion under advisement."

"You know, all women like long poky things, but they don't have to be attached to the body for extreme satisfaction."

Cyn stepped between us. "Are you two talking about sex *again*?"

"What makes you say that?"

"Long poky things? What else could you be talking about?"

"Weapons class. Swords, daggers, spears, tridents, dildos."

Alyze snorted.

Cyn glared at me. Judgement rolled off her. "You're a bad influence on her. You should be ashamed of yourself."

"Don't even try shaming me. Alyze was no angel when we met her. At least, underwater she wasn't."

"Don't remind me," Alyze whined before straightening. "Let's hit the lake later."

I gestured to our dear siren friend. "If anything, she's corrupting me."

Alyze waved as she entered her room. "Listen, honey, you do you, and I'll do . . ." she grinned and slammed the door before she could finish.

Cyn gasped.

"Oh, don't play the V card with me. You already dished about the old boyfriend back at Sweet Valley High."

Her tales only further confirmed that he had deserved to die. The selfish prick.

"That's what I get for drinking with you. Never again." She pulled out her key and unlocked our door. We'd taken to locking it all the time. Locking the door spelled it from unwanted intruders, and with the whole Goldwell situation, we chose to take at least that precaution.

"You say that now, but we both know that's a lie. You loved every minute of hanging out with Alyze, Red, and your dear old sis."

She snorted as she walked into the room. "Confession time. I never bonded with my friends from high school. I always felt out of step."

I patted her on the back as I stepped past her. "Now you know why."

She flopped onto her bed and sighed. "I do. I haven't entirely accepted this new life of mine, but I really like everyone I've met. I'm not sure about the classes, though."

I tugged on a black sweater with the yellow Air symbol embroidered on it and plopped onto my own bed. "What do you mean? I'd take Weapons Training over Potion Making any day of the week and twice on Sunday."

"I'd give anything to make potions. I loved chemistry. Weapons however . . . not so much."

"Afraid of sharp pointy things?" I grinned.

She rolled her eyes. "I'm not talking about sex, Dez." She sounded tired.

"I know. What makes it so hard? No pun intended."

She sat up and bent her legs, dropping her hands on her folded knees. Meditation class was no problem for her. "I wasn't exactly physically gifted or into sports in high school."

"But you're a vampire now. A Sempiternal, no less. You

154

are naturally blessed with physical abilities, though you evidently didn't use them before you changed."

She sent a pointed gaze over at me. "Before you killed me."

I rolled my eyes, lying back against my pillow. I wasn't having this conversation again. Whenever Cyn got down or was cranky, she'd attack me about forcing her to change early. I still didn't know unequivocally if she was a turned vampire or a born one, but over the last couple of weeks, she'd appeared to be in full control of her bloodlust.

She groaned from her bed. "Weapons Training is hard. I ache in places I didn't think could ache."

"I ache in places too," I said sadly, still unsatisfied after my merman.

"I'm not talking about sex, Dez," she snapped.

I sat up to look at her. "I know. You're tired. It's new. Your dislike for Weapons class is similar to my dislike of Potion Making. They make us take classes we're not as strong in. You know that."

"Anastasia is strong in everything."

"She is one of the strongest of our class, but she still has a lot to learn. She was raised knowing she'd one day attend Silverwood Academy, and her mom schooled her on the basics, but like I said, she is only *one* of the strongest. Do you remember our guard at Silverwood Prison?"

"I try not to."

"Right, well, he called us the most dangerous inmates there."

"Because we're Sempiternals?"

"That and sisters. Think about it. The potency of our individual abilities are amplified when we're together, like during our Elemental Training sessions. Together, we kick everyone's ass in our ability to command the elements.

We're two of the strongest in our class. We are powerful. We are fearsome. We are forces to be reckoned with." I sprang up from my bed, an idea coming to me.

"What is it?"

I rushed to the door. "I'll be right back."

"Dez, wait!" she shouted, but I was already down the hall. I had to speak to Jace.

I BARGED into the meditation studio and hurried to Jace's bedroom door. It was only ten, but I was banking on him being there. I thought about knocking, then decided against it. I was too impatient. I swung the door open, rushed in, and smacked into a tall, muscular chest.

"Ooof." Strong, long arms wrapped around me. "Deziree," he sighed, as if he'd been waiting for me all along.

His sexy, earthy scent filled my nostrils, and I immediately relaxed. This . . . this was what I longed for. Whatever other reason I came here was completely forgotten.

Suddenly, his body stiffened, and I didn't mean that in a good way. He broke away from me. "Dez, what are you doing here?"

Instinctively, my body drifted toward him. He shifted back, putting more distance between us.

That itch returned, worse than before. "Come on, Jace, you know you want me."

He lifted his hand to stop me. "You shouldn't be here."

"You were on your way out. It's your fault we collided."

He blinked rapidly, trying to come up with an explanation. "My studio alarm was tripped. I was on my way to see who it was."

I sidled closer to him. "I thought those alarms prevented people from entering unless you wanted them to come in." I altered the words a bit to suit the situation, but now that I said them, I also knew it was the truth.

He cleared his throat. I continued my advance, my eyes never leaving his as he backed deeper into his room until his bed blocked his path. Or maybe it was where he intended to go all along. Without speaking, I pushed him down on the bed, my body splitting his knees apart as I edged closer. His hands wrapped around the back of my legs and found their way up my hips. It was all the invitation I needed. No more flirting. No more stolen glances. No more resistance. Just me, him, and our soon-to-be naked bodies tumbling together.

I perched my hands on his shoulders as I swung one leg, then the other, over his thighs, straddling him. All the while my purple eyes never left his gold ones, as if fused together into one singular desire. A shadow of hesitation crossed his face when I edged up toward him, but then my lady bits hit his man parts. Our combined moans replaced any remaining uncertainty. I bit my lip, shifting my hips side to side, settling deeper onto him. Our lips hovered a breath's width apart. We were both playing a game.

A low, possessive growl traveled up his chest as his hands gripped my ass and tugged me closer.

Game over.

Our lips crashed together. Literal sparks exploded between us as our opposing energies joined into one. Hands found skin, leading to more skin. The room flooded with the sounds of ripping and tearing fabric. When relieved of all my clothing, I pressed my wetness against him. More growls erupted. His. Mine. Ours.

Fingers tangled in hair. Tongue warred with tongue. More moans. Groans. Exquisite sighs.

Bodies pressing together. Wanting. Needing. Desiring.

He gripped my ass and lifted me above his hard dick. My slick folds dripped for him. Ached for him. Pulsed for him. The itch I needed scratched.

His length speared into me as he brought me down on him. Our bodies colliding again and again and again. Climbing. Climbing. Climbing toward the highest peak. Losing ourselves as our bodies joined together, ever climbing, ever seeking, ever peaking.

His nails dug into my ass. Mine dug into his back. Ensuring we both got where we needed to go.

Screams of "Yes, yes, YES," filled the room as the peak loomed ever closer. His, mine, ours.

So close . . .

Yet, not close enough . . .

Ever elusive . . .

But almost . . .

More "Yeses."

More climbing.

More everything.

Until finally . . .

Fireworks exploding. Pussy pulsing. Length throbbing. Climaxing. Spiraling. Again, and again, and again.

Until we were spent.

Then we went again.

And again.

And again.

CHAPTER
TWENTY-TWO

ez

MY HIPS SASHAYED side to side as I walked back to my room. Everything inside me thrummed in the best of ways. The ache I'd had for weeks was finally sated. I'd had more sex during that period than I'd had in a lifetime, yet it wasn't until tonight that everything fit into place. Everything had happened exactly how it was meant to.

We didn't speak after. Exhaustion overtook us both, and we collapsed in a tangled heap of arms and legs. A needling in the back of my head woke me. Not a desire for more sex, but a feeling, a knowing, that something was wrong. I considered waking Jace to let him know I was leaving, but he slept so peacefully. So beautifully. All hesitation was erased from his face.

I moaned again as I swaggered down the hall. I'd just seen two of my past liaisons, but I hardly spared them a glance. They weren't terrible. Some had performed quite admirably, actually, but no one came close to Jace's level.

Fire burned between us. Jace's Silver Cloak tattoo on his back included all the elements. Only the most powerful brothers and sister bore the marks of all of them. Most mastered one or two aside from their own, but few mastered Spirit, Air, Water, Earth, and Fire.

"Hey, Dez, looking to knock some boots tonight?" drawled a guy from his doorway. I couldn't remember his name. His attempt at dominance during sex hadn't worked for me. He'd wanted to take rather than provide equal enjoyment. I had flipped him over on his ass, tried to get mine in, and he blew his load after two strokes. That was actually my nickname for him: Two Strokes.

"Hey, Two Strokes, I'm good. More than good," I purred, still feeling the aftereffects of multiple orgasms erupt in me.

"Why do you call me Two Strokes?"

Gods, he really was a fucking idiot. I spared a quick glance over my shoulder. "Would you rather Two-Second Man?"

His face scrunched, and he slammed the door.

Guess he finally figured out the meaning of his nickname. Took some people a while, and those were usually the ones who wound up failing out of Silverwood Academy. Only those with the best brains, physical prowess, and heart made it through to join Silver Dagger Sisterhood or Silver Cloak Brotherhood. Maybe that's what made Jace so intriguing to me. I knew what I was getting into with him.

I shook my head. No, I hated to admit it, but there was something more than tantalizing tattoos and a finely chiseled physique.

Silverwood Academy proved everything I wanted it to be and more, and Jace was a delicious addition to it. I was ill-suited for long-term commitment, but one-night stands, or several-night stands, definitely multiple-orgasm-night stands, fit in just fine with my present and future lifestyle. Yes, Jace would serve me well.

I glanced up at the hallway ceiling outside the bedroom I shared with my sister. The artificial stars beamed down at me from the night sky. I smiled at them. The founders of Silverwood Academy wanted us to embrace the "As above, so below" concept, bringing the outside inside. The magickally enhanced ceiling was one method.

That bad feeling took hold in my brain again, and it wouldn't let go. I pushed open my bedroom door to find Cyn wrapped tighter than a condom around an ephemeral, and he didn't look so good.

Crap.

When I first entered the Change, before the Guardians found me, I had feasted on several ephemerals who'd offered their necks to me. As a Sempiternal, I was the Elvis Presley of vampires. I now found the vamp-obsessed humans boring and lacking the vitality necessary to sustain me, given their whole sharing-is-caring life motto. Apparently my sister didn't possess the same dislike for them.

Of course, she didn't know better. After her change, she went right to Silverwood Prison. Stale blood bags at mealtimes paled in comparison to the real thing.

Silverwood Academy didn't have many humans, being that it's a school dedicated to training future Silver Dagger Sisterhood and Silver Cloak Brotherhood members, but leave it to Sis to find one.

I shook my head at the situation before me, unsure if I was proud or disgusted. For all her complaining about me killing her and her whining about not being able to go to college, she didn't seem to harbor any regrets hindering her from becoming a capable and deadly vampire, a proud Sempiternal through and through.

I should be happy I had found my long-lost sister in the backwater town in bum-fucked western Kentucky and given her immortality early, but right now, with her sucking the life out of the ephemeral—on my favorite chair no less—not so much. To make matters worse, if my sister wound up killing him, she'd be in direct violation of one of the school's only rules, and when one of those rules was broken, it spelled trouble, including another trip through Silverwood Prison, and this time I wouldn't be able to go with her. The Council made that very clear during my hearing. Third time, dagger to the heart.

"Cyn," I hissed, trying to keep my voice down so I didn't alert our neighbors, all with varying degrees of enhanced hearing and smell.

I stalked over. "Cyn, let go."

But she hung on to the ephemeral's neck like she was slurping chocolate at an all-you-can-eat buffet. She tested my not-so-good patience.

"Cyn."

When she failed to respond, I grabbed a handful of her hair and yanked. As soon as she released her mouth from the ephemeral's neck, I threw her across the room where she smashed into the wall and fell in a crumpled heap to the floor.

She sat up in a euphoric daze from the overdose. "Wow, that was amazing. Better than sex."

I put my hands on my hips. "Do I need to explain the Sempiternal Code or review the school's rules again? Apparently you've forgotten both of them."

She swiped her sleeve across her blood-stained lips. "Please do."

The sight of fresh blood made my mouth tingle, but I wouldn't let myself get distracted by it. We drew our strength from someone's energy. Blood just added a spicy component to it, and evidently, Cyn liked spice. This surprised me. Prior to her transition, she wore shirts up to her chin with little to no skin showing. She could have passed for a nun. Much different from the corset with the plunging bustline she wore now.

I studied the corset closer. My corset, and it was ripped down the front. The torn fabric fueled my rage. I'd lead off on a tirade about the Sempiternal Code, jump to Silverwood Academy rules, and end with a lecture on borrowing things without asking. But then I heard a moan, and all my attention shifted.

In my anger, I'd forgotten about the ephemeral. I glanced over and realized it was Canyon from Herbology, Cyn's flavor of the month at the start of the year. This was not good. He was a favorite at the Academy. I think it had something to do with his light green eyes in contrast to his dark skin that attracted people to him. But now, as he sat dazed in the chair, there was an aura around him. It was weak—I could only see it because his defenses were down in his depleted state, but it was there nonetheless. Someone in his family tree had gotten freaky with a supernatural. That much was certain.

"Go heal him," I hissed at my sister.

"Naw," she drawled, her southern accent maxing out in her blood high. "I don't want to ruin my buzz."

"So you want me to pool from my own resources? How do you know I'm not depleted?"

Cyn stood up, adjusted her corset to ensure ample breast exposure, which with the tear was not a problem, and stalked out of the room.

"Where are you going?"

"To party. Don't wait up."

"You're leaving?"

"Yes, I am," she said, the door slamming behind her.

Canyon moaned again. I cursed my sister. Aside from a little misstep with Canyon on her first day, she'd done well . . . making friends, excelling in her classes. She even possessed a knack for ferreting out the evil demon in Demonology, which I wished they'd update the name of since not all demons are bad, but I digress. Just recently, she'd stood out in Weapons Training. I was proud of her. She'd finally begun to demonstrate that she'd make a good partner for me when we took over the family business. And now, look at this mess.

"Hey, Dez," Canyon whispered. "I'm not feeling so good."

I knelt down in front of him. "You're not looking so good either."

His aura shimmered around him. I loathed the idea of entering it.

"Canyon, what are you?"

He closed his eyes as if about to fall into an eternal sleep. I'd have to hurry if I didn't want to expend too much of my energy on him. If an evil warlock attacked me, I'd be screwed.

He smacked his lips together. "What do you mean?"

I debated whether to mention the aura or not. He was so vanquished it was likely that I could just compel him to forget our conversation along with my sister draining him, even if he had been drinking vervain. I traced my fingers along the edges of his aura. "You have a magickal shield."

"Like Captain America." He grinned, his eyes still closed.

"No, that was made of metal. An aura shimmers around you."

He peeked a lone green eye open. My entire body tingled. I didn't expect it to react in such a way to Canyon. It must have been the magick.

"Are you serious?"

"Is your dad or mom or maybe some distant relative fae?"

He peeked both eyes open. "Faerie? You think I'm a faerie?"

Again my body reacted to him. I hated myself and him for this physical attraction. I must have been weak. I needed to find someone to feed off of, but not Jace. Couldn't take a chance with Jace since I already felt things for him I shouldn't.

"Forget I said anything. Forget Cyn fed off you. Forget everything that happened tonight."

I bit my wrist and shoved it into his mouth.

yn

I COLLAPSED against the wall outside our bedroom door. When Dez ripped me off Canyon, I was relieved and more than a little bit appreciative. One minute, Canyon and I were studying Herbology and the next, I was on his lap on Dez's chair. It had started as kissing, but I soon began drawing his energy. It was the most intoxicating thing I'd ever experienced. I couldn't get enough of it. Canyon didn't help matters. He caressed my breasts, throwing me into some kind of hormonal frenzy. My fangs emerged, and he traced the tips with his tongue. So freaking hot. Soon after, he began sucking on my neck, and then I was sucking his. He shoved his neck deeper into my mouth, as if tempting me to bite him, so I did. Contrary to what Dez probably thought about life as a Sempiternal, I didn't want to feed off a person's blood or his energy in order to live, but some-

166

thing had come over me. I sucked on his neck until I felt his life flicker. Then I sucked some more. I couldn't stop. Lucky for Canyon—and me, I guess—Dez walked in when she did. Otherwise, his story would have ended abruptly, and mine would end with a silver stake to the heart.

These last few weeks, I'd prided myself on making the transition to vampire, the life I never asked for, smoothly. I excelled in my classes. Professors loved me. I even suspected Dez was a tad jealous of my success. She had turned me for companionship, and so that the two of us, once we got into Silver Dagger Sisterhood, could carry on the family business, hunting and killing rogue supernaturals, whether with a twist of his neck or a stake to her heart or some other diabolical means we hadn't been taught yet. I think she sometimes questioned her decision to kill me, though she'd never admit that to anyone, let alone me. After my actions tonight, I didn't blame her.

I listened to her whispering to Canyon on the other side of the door. She asked him what he was. What did she mean by that? He was a boy. Okay, a man. A very attractive man. But he was human. An ephemeral, as Dez called them. As if Canyon and other humans ranked lower in the hierarchy of life—most likely in case an unfortunate accident took place during a consensual feeding session. I guess I understood that point of view after what I'd almost done to Canyon.

But there had been something different about him tonight. The first time I bit him, the day after my induction into the Academy, I could control my bloodlust. Well, after biting him, anyway. The point is, I didn't drain him. And since then, we'd hung out in the potions lab, we'd studied together. Never was I drawn to him like I was tonight.

I glanced down at my barely covered chest. I didn't even

remember putting on the corset. Of course, it was Dez's. And it was torn. Shit. I'd get to deal with her wrath later along with my own self-loathing.

I took a deep breath and swallowed hard, gathering the courage to walk down the hallway with my boobs hanging out.

"At least your nipples are covered," Dez, who had no problem with public nudity, would say.

I could do this. I could do this.

"Hey, Cyn, let's see what's beneath that piece of fabric," someone taunted.

Any other day, any other time, I'd turn around and verbally attack the assailant for his sexual harassment monkey-brain comment, but not today. Today I needed to get away or I'd explode, and no one wanted to witness that shit show.

More catcalls followed me. I ignored them and burst through the double doors. For more than two hundred years, emerging Sempiternals, along with other newly turned supernaturals, found safe haven inside the star-shaped stone building of Silverwood Academy, but not me. The school felt like another form of prison. My sister had made a choice for me that I would never have made on my own.

"You were going to go through the Change anyway, once you came of age," she'd said to me dozens of times as a form of apology, but I didn't believe her. How could I? I'd lived a normal human existence for almost two decades with no hint of magick, no sense of the supernatural what-soever. Then, she'd crashed my "mom's" car and I'd woken up to a new life.

My feet landed on the soft pine needles as I ran along the familiar path to the one place on campus I found refuge.

The darkness of the night used to alarm me. I was terrified of the monsters under the bed.

I was the monster now.

I leapt over the split rail fence. My feet landed in the dew-covered grass. I gasped in relief as the wetness seeped into my bare soles. I needed this. I needed to be here. I tore across the field. Soft neighs and nickers greeted me. When I found the middle of the herd, I threw back my head and screamed, punching at the night sky, tears streaming down my face. "It's not fair!"

The horses didn't startle or take off at my outburst. Since my second night at Silverwood, when I'd stumbled upon this herd of wild horses in Wildwood Preserves, they had become my constant. They'd grown used to my loud ways.

"It's not fair! I'm supposed to go to college. I'm supposed to be human. I'm supposed to fall in love. To die one day," I sobbed.

As my screams entered the void and I had nothing left to give, I collapsed into a heap. The moon and horses were the only witnesses to my tantrum. I clawed at the intense ache in my chest. Could a heart burst from so much pain? It felt like it could.

I'd almost killed Canyon. Almost sucked the life energy out of another human being. The blood made it better. An aphrodisiac.

I could never lose myself like that again. I couldn't lose what humanity I had left.

Juniper pushed her nose into my cheek, pulling me out of myself. My hand found the patch of fur beneath her chin and scratched. She folded down next to me. Of all the horses, Juniper was my favorite. A white mare who glowed in the darkness as if from supernatural foundations. For all I knew, she could be.

I lay across her middle, giving her belly and withers attention. The soft chewing and shifting of the rest of the herd soothed me better than any person ever could.

Crunching leaves yanked my attention away from Juniper and toward the Wildwoods from which I came. The other horses fell silent, also sensing the presence of another. I swallowed the lump in my throat, fearing a rogue supernatural had found me. The magickal boundary was supposed to prevent unwanted visitors from entering the grounds, but I found that hard to believe. Magick was strong, but after my extracurricular research over the last few weeks, I knew how powerful Maleficium could be. Every muscle tensed as I shifted away from Juniper to stand. She remained relaxed and folded on the ground.

So, not a predator then. As lead mare, she'd protect her herd if danger existed. I squinted into the dark wood, trying to make out who or what was watching me. A soft glow emerged, growing larger and larger, yet approaching slowly, ever elusive to my sight. Juniper lifted her head and whinnied. She rose to her feet, her body quivering with excitement, but she remained at my side, steadying me.

A beautiful white horse approached, majestic and powerful, carrying a rider upon its back. I couldn't make out who it was he carried, but if Juniper wasn't alarmed, then neither was I. I was a monster after all.

"No, you are not," a woman's voice echoed across the field as if I had said my thought aloud.

The rest of the herd neighed and snorted loudly in greeting and took off toward the white stallion and his rider. Juniper remained ever steadfast by my side.

I watched the horse and rider approach, surrounded by

the herd. The rider reached down and scratched the muzzles of each horse welcoming her.

I blinked a few times, unable to believe my eyes. The energy and the blood must have addled my brain because before me could not be who I believed it was.

"Hello, Cynda. I'm glad to finally meet you."

I stood dumbfounded, unable to react, until finally I found my voice and murmured more to myself than to her. "Goddess Rhiannon?"

She smiled, her face glowing in the darkness. "Rhiannon is just fine."

"Wh-what are you doing here?"

She slid off her horse, landing softly in the grass, her bare feet also absorbing the dew.

"Meeting you, of course."

I pulled my hand to my heart, unable to speak.

"Yes, you."

"Why? I'm a monster."

She laughed, her head swinging back and forth. "You are no more a monster than I am, as all children are, as all living beings are. You were at the Induction. Do you remember the beauty, the magick, on the night of the ceremony?"

Of course I remembered the evening. I remembered everything about it. It was one of the most meaningful memories of my new life since Dez had turned me. Juniper nudged her muzzle into my shoulder. I reached up and scratched under her chin again.

But something about Rhiannon's answer bothered me. "You didn't pick me, though."

"No, I didn't. But not because I didn't want to. Lilith wanted to keep you and your sister together. I agreed with her. She has much to teach you, as do the rest of my sisters, but you found my special herd of horses, and they selected you as one of their own."

I rubbed Juniper's neck, avoiding Rhiannon's gaze. Her ethereal beauty shone so brightly in the night sky that it was difficult to gaze upon her for long, especially with the weight of her confession. It was a compliment to the highest degree.

"It is a compliment to the highest degree," she echoed me.

"It's rude to intrude on another's thoughts," I snapped at her, immediately regretting it.

She threw back her head and barked at the moon. "Lilith chose well. Your spark will shine brightly, even at your darkest moments." Suddenly she was in front of me. "So will this," she said, leaning over and kissing my fore-head. She rested her hand upon my shoulder, the spot still tingling. "Child, I do not visit often, but my companions will always come to assist you. Be well and know that you will serve a Great Purpose."

TWENTY-FOUR

 yn

I WALKED BACK to my room feeling lighter, more full of possibility. Rhiannon had visited me. Me. She claimed she had wanted me for her own, and I believed her. She'd no reason to lie. She was a goddess for goddess's sake. She answered to no one, except maybe Mother Earth and Father Sky. My forehead tingled where she had kissed it and proclaimed that I would serve a Great Purpose. What that purpose was, I didn't know, and honestly, I didn't relish finding out anytime soon. School, life, and bloodlust were complicated enough to handle.

Speaking of which, I had my sister to answer to. I should probably check on Canyon too, though I wouldn't mind putting that off for a while . . . or forever.

The hallway's ceiling reflected the dawning of the new day. I'd spent more time with Rhiannon than I realized.

With any luck, Dez was asleep, and her lecture would have to wait.

I quietly opened the door and tiptoed in. Vampires, especially Sempiternals, moved superfast. But when needed, we could also move slower than a human, and that's exactly what I did so I wouldn't wake my sister. I edged over to my bed, careful not to even glance at her for fear she'd feel my eyes upon her and wake as a result.

My big fluffy pillow and cozy comforter called to me, and after the long night I'd had, I couldn't wait to reunite with them. The old bed frame creaked. In the dead silence, it sounded like a gunshot.

"Trying to evade me?" Dez purred, shooting from her bed and hopping onto mine.

"If I said yes, would you let me get some sleep?"

Her purple eyes flashed in the darkness. "Not a chance. I've been waiting for you so we could have a little chat."

"Great. Can't wait."

She slapped her hand on my blanketed leg. "Saucy. I like it." She shifted closer. "What's that on your forehead?"

My hand reached for the spot Rhiannon had kissed. It was still warm. "What?"

"Right where your fingers are. What is it?" She leaned closer. Personal space meant nothing to her. "It looks like a crescent moon."

I flung the covers off and ran to the vanity mirror. Dez was right. A small crescent moon glowed from my forehead along with three faint shining stars. I pressed it, even tried to wipe it off, but it remained exactly the same size and brightness no matter what I did.

"Where did you get it?" Dez peeked over my shoulder. "Is it from sucking the life energy from Canyon?"

My defenses immediately went up. The beauty of

Rhiannon's crescent moon kiss wouldn't be corrupted with the toxicity of bloodlust.

"No, it's not," I growled.

"Easy." She backed away with her hands up. "Don't get your hackles up."

Hackles? What was she saying? I wasn't a dog or a wolf shifter. "No hackles here."

"It's just an expression. Don't you think I know you're not a shifter of the furry kind? We're sisters for goddess's sake."

"Speaking of goddesses, Rhiannon kissed my forehead and left this mark."

"You went out to your special field again? I should have gone after you, but I had your Canyon mess to clean up."

"Hold up. You know where I go?"

She rolled her eyes. "Do you really think I'd let my newbie vampire sister go gallivanting off in the woods in the middle of the night without supervision?"

"Yes, actually. I'm an adult, and you need to start treating me like one," I said, trying not to sound like a petulant child, which would completely discredit my argument.

"I get it. I remember turning eighteen and thinking that I was an adult. But the thing is, I grew up hunting monsters and spent much of my life alone. I'd seen far more of the world by the time I turned eighteen than someone who lived a sheltered life without any knowledge that the supernatural world even existed."

I opened my mouth to argue, but she threw her hand up and energy-closed it.

"I wasn't a newbie vampire at eighteen either. I didn't change until last spring. You've got a lot more stuff to deal with."

I narrowed my eyes at her. "And whose fault is that?"

She pulled her hand to her chest. "Mine. It's mine. I went through the Change to become a Sempiternal, got sent to Silverwood Prison where I finally got a lead on the whereabouts of my little sister after a decade of searching, and took action. Forgive me for caring." She jumped off the bed, stormed over to hers, and slid under the covers.

"You spent ten years looking for me?"

She huffed. "More than that. As soon as I processed that my little sister wasn't going to live with us, I started asking Dad questions, but his lips were sealed on the subject of your whereabouts." She sat up. "Wait a second . . ."

I hurried over to her bed and hopped on. "What?"

Her purple eyes studied me as her fingers played with her chin. "I wonder . . ."

"What?"

"I'll be right back." She slid out of bed.

"Where are you going?"

She stopped. "Well, I was going to ask Jace, but that conversation might get complicated. I'll go find Professor Logan."

"What happened with Jace?"

"And I should probably shower," she added, ignoring me.

"Why don't you just talk it through with me? I'm the one who gave you the idea."

She breathed in and out of her nose, as if considering my offer. "You're a newbie."

"I'm not completely new, and I *am* your sister."

She stood watching me for several long minutes without blinking. If she weren't my sister, it would be creepy. Actually, she was my sister, and it was still creepy. Finally, after much too long, she said, "I think the reason

Dad never talked about your whereabouts was because he was spelled not to."

I frowned at her. "By whom? Why?"

She climbed back up in her bed. "I don't know, but it makes sense. He always reminded me to train my sister, but when I asked where you were, he'd blank out like he didn't know who I was talking about."

"Maybe he put me out of his mind so it didn't hurt so much," I offered, though it physically pained me to say it.

She played with her chin again. "Maybe . . . but that doesn't feel true. How did the words feel when they came out of your mouth?"

I raised my eyebrows. "Sister thing?"

She shook her head. "Intuition. Our sister bonds aren't that tight yet since we were kept apart for so many years." Her eyes rounded, and she slammed her hand down. "That's it."

"What? Words. Use your words. And, yes, the words felt wrong when they came out of my mouth."

She wagged her finger as she leaned in. I joined her, and we were so close we were almost kissing. She tilted her head to the side and whispered. "I think we were kept apart for a reason."

"Why?"

"Remember how Jace said we shouldn't tell anyone about Lilith?"

"Yeah, but he never gave a reason, did he? Other than they don't intermingle with students much."

She shook her head.

"What about Rhiannon's mark on my forehead? Won't people ask questions about that?"

She pulled away and lifted her thumbs up to my forehead without touching it. "May I?"

"I can't believe you actually asked."

"I take the rules of the Academy very seriously."

I raised an eyebrow at her.

She grinned. "Well, mostly."

Her thumbs gently pushed into the mark with the rest of her fingers rimming the moon without directly touching it. I wasn't sure how I knew that, but I did.

"Energy vibrates off it."

"I can feel it."

She pulled her lips into her mouth as she studied the mark, her thumbs lightly skimming it. "I don't know if it'll be visible during the day. Maybe there's a spell we could use to hide it."

It felt wrong to hide a gift from a goddess. Rhiannon wouldn't have left it if she felt it put me in danger. "No spells. No makeup."

She dropped her hands. "But, Cyn . . ."

"No. Rhiannon wouldn't do something that would hurt me."

Her chest rose and fell, her eyes never leaving the crescent. "You're probably right."

Truth vibrated in me. I raised my chest, straightening my back. "I *am* right."

The side of her lip curved up, and a dimple popped out. "Alrighty then. I'll talk to Jace about it."

"You really trust him, don't you?"

Her gaze met mine. "I really do, which feels weird to me on so many levels. Dad drilled into me to never trust anyone. Yet, with Jace I do. Professor Logan too, but my relationship with him is different. More of an uncle-niece thing versus what I have with Jace."

"Could Jace be compelling you or using some sort of magick on you?"

"That would make sense, wouldn't it? But I don't think so. Something exists between us."

"Aside from out-of-control horniness?"

She snorted. "Yes, aside from that. I'm drawn to him, and I don't know why. I don't even know what he is."

Her response reminded me of her earlier conversation with Canyon. "What is Canyon? Is he fae?"

She shook her head back and forth. "I don't know." Then she grinned, her eyes glowing with that mischievous twinkle of hers. "You were listening, weren't you?"

There was no point denying I overhead them. "Yes. I needed a few minutes to recover."

"So, the blasé attitude about almost killing him?"

In the dark of the room, it was easier to share secrets, to confess truths, to build our sister bond.

"Was an act. I was freaked out. I didn't know what had come over me. One second he was in my room, asking if I wanted to study."

"Then the next you were sucking out his life energy."

"Pretty much."

She leaned back in. "Was he spelled?"

I closed my eyes and listened to my intuition. Between mindfulness classes since elementary school and Jace's meditation sessions, I was set. Or so I thought. But the thing was, when it came to Canyon there was a blank space surrounding him.

She gave me what she thought was adequate time, and in her gentle, not-so-gentle manner, she broke my meditation. "Usually a yes or no answer."

"I don't know. I can't tell. You saw him too. Was he?"

She closed her eyes as she drew her lips into her mouth again, but there was nothing calm about her process. Her nostrils kept flaring in and out.

"I thought it was a yes or no answer."

She opened her eyes. "It's cloudy. I remember exactly what I did before entering our room, and let me tell you, the sex was super yummy and hot." She closed her eyes. "Goddess, so fucking hot. But then, nothing—at least not when it comes to Canyon."

"So, I guess that means ..."

"He must have been. Maybe he doesn't have supernatural blood at all. Maybe someone cast a spell over him."

"But who?"

She snapped her fingers. "Wait a second, he's an ephemeral, so he's related to either someone from Silver Dagger Sisterhood or the Brotherhood?" She fell deep into thought again, but she overlooked the obvious answer.

"Or his mom's a professor here."

She pinned me in place with her intense glare, her nostrils flaring again. "I forgot all about Goldwell. Shit."

ez

ONCE AGAIN I regretted turning my sister. Don't get me wrong. We'd bonded in the darkness discussing Rhiannon's mark, why someone would spell our dad not to remember who he gave Cynda to, along with my sister almost killing Canyon. She knew to stay away from Professor Goldwell, but she had ignored me about Canyon. How many other times had they seen each other without my knowledge? How many times had he stopped over to study when I was out prowling the halls? I found it hard to believe last night was the first time Cyn had gone too far since her little incident with Canyon the day after the Induction Ceremony. She couldn't be trusted, especially with her bloodlust surfacing again, though she seemed more in control of herself after Rhiannon.

Canyon's green eyes were beautiful, but Silverwood

dripped with sexy wolf shifters, Sempiternals, and other supernaturals who were also beautiful and a lot harder to kill.

"Argh," I yelled in frustration on my way to breakfast. Between my lack of sleep and my disappointment in Cynda, I was in desperate need of caffeine and nourishment. I had burned a shit-ton of calories getting sexed up with Jace, and I was probably dehydrated too. I didn't drink from Jace. Blood exchanged during sex could bind two people together. I didn't want to be bound to him or anyone else, except myself and my goddess, of course.

"You had sex, didn't you?" Alyze asked, catching up to me.

"I always have sex."

"Yes, but you've got swagger."

"I've always got swagger."

"True, but you smell different." She leaned in and sniffed my neck. "Who was it?" She inhaled again. "What was it?"

"Ew, gross," I snapped, waving her away from me. "I showered."

"You don't stink like sweat and sex. You've been marked."

I hit the brakes. "Marked?"

Alyze pulled her hands to her chest. "I'm a siren."

"Yeah, and . . ."

"Morrigan is my goddess. Water is my element, but as a siren, I have a close affinity to Maeve."

"Tell me something I don't know. What do you mean 'marked'?" I spun around, looking at my body. I didn't see any type of marking, and my forehead didn't have a crescent moon on it like my sister's. (Which had disappeared in the daylight—I checked before I left. I couldn't completely abandon her, even if she pissed me off.)

"Through the years, Maeve married many kings before abandoning them for the hunt. Some supernatural. Some not."

I twirled my finger in the air for her to hurry the fuck up. She dipped her mouth to my ear.

"She never let any of them mark her, because she didn't want to become the hunted."

Shivers ran down my spine. "What do you mean 'hunted'?" My dad never mentioned anything about being marked, and I'd never read anything about it. I was the hunter, damn it. That was the family business.

"Well, for Maeve, she saw the mark as a permanent tie to someone, and she didn't want anything permanent."

I respected that desire. I liked having sex with Jace, but I didn't want anything long-lasting. Anything permanent. That was the reason I didn't bite him.

"The mark allows two-way connection."

"Meaning?"

"You will always know where the other one is. No matter what realm you enter. No matter who else you might intermingle with."

A tsunami of anger rose up in me. "What are you saying?"

"Maeve didn't want anyone to track her movements."

Me neither.

"Is there a way to sever it?"

She held her hands up. "I don't know. I can search the library or ask Professor Logan?"

"No, don't involve him, but check the library. And, Alyze?" I squeezed her hands. Her eyes widened in surprise then dilated as I compelled her. "Don't tell anyone. Keep it between us."

I felt a twinge of guilt compelling my friend, but not enough to stop. Her pupils narrowed to pinpricks before filling her irises. "I won't."

I released her and vamp-sped away. Jace had some explaining to do.

⬤

I FLUNG open Jace's studio door. Scattered bodies lay littered across the floor. Every single one of them sat up at my entrance. They might be in a meditation session, but fighting was in their blood. Their bones. That's why they attended Silverwood Academy.

Jace's lips rose when he saw me, before he carefully changed his composure into that of anger.

"Miss Wickershim, what is the meaning of this interruption?"

I prowled over to him. *Him* the prey, *me* the hunter, regardless of whatever shit he'd pulled last night.

"I'm sorry. Should I have *marked* my entrance differently?"

He dropped his gaze, clearing his throat. "Class, we will adjourn for today. We'll pick up where we left off next time."

"Make sure to *mark* your calendars."

I crossed my arms and narrowed my eyes at Jace as his students filed out of the room. Some cast curious glances my way, but I seared them with my bitch aura, which I had possessed long before I'd changed into a vampire. When the studio door closed, I sped over and locked it before advancing within inches of him.

"Explain."

He swallowed, running his hands through his hair. My fingers longed to feather back those luscious, silky locks for him. His gaze wandered around the studio as if searching for someone, anyone, to save him.

"I'm right here."

His eyes met mine. "I know, Deziree. Gods, I know."

"Right, because of that marking thingy. My chest is vibrating along with the rest of me. What the hell did you do to me, Jace?"

His eyes dropped to my lips, and he licked his. I tracked the movement. The wetness of them doing things to my body counterproductive to the intense rage I came here with.

"What did you do to me, Jace?" I murmured, the anger disappearing into something else. Something far more primal.

His nostrils flared, scenting my mood shift. It triggered something inside me. Something I couldn't stop even if I wanted to. I flung my arms and legs around him. He gripped my ass, pressing me against his very hard dick, and slammed me into the wall. I cried out in surprise. His eyes went to mine in concern, thinking he had hurt me, but he didn't. If anything, he spurred me on to wanting him more. Hard and fast, just how I liked it. I captured his lips, plunging my tongue into his open mouth.

My nails dug into his back, drawing us tighter together. Too many layers of fabric existed between us. He came to the same realization. He released my ass, letting my legs drop, his lips never leaving mine. He yanked off my leggings as I tugged off his yoga pants. His clothing choices for his profession came in handy. No buttons, no zippers. I wrapped my hand around his full length, stroking him. His fingers trailed up my inner thigh to my slick folds, plunging in and out, teasing my clit, spiraling me to that peak.

"Come for me, Deziree," he breathed into my mouth, and I did. Intense, sharp, hard, and wanting more. I wrapped my leg around his, pressing myself against him. He took my invitation, grabbing my ass cheeks as I wrapped my other leg around him. He pressed me against the wall. Pinned in place, he locked my hands in his and flung them above my head. At his mercy, he drove into me, again, and again, and again, rekindling the fire in my clit to join him on the journey. And I did, climbing quickly to new heights with him. Winding ever higher and higher until finally . . .

"Now," I cried out, and he obliged, peaking that fucking mountain with me. Convulsing. Pulsing. Spasming.

Both spent, his forehead dropped to mine, our chests heaving as we fought to catch our breath. Entwined together, we collapsed to the floor with him still inside me.

My heart raced in time to his. My entire body thrummed with ecstasy. I didn't know sex could be so fucking yummy. Enjoyable, yes. Stimulating, absolutely. But yummy? Now I knew and would never be the same. I was forever changed. Forever marked . . .

Shit. That's what had brought me here in the first place. I shifted my hips to pull him out of me, his limpness immediately hardening as it slapped against me while I pushed down his thighs. His chest rumbled with that same possessive growl as last night. I groaned in reply before remembering myself and inching farther away from him.

"What did you do to me, Jace?"

His lips traveled along my neck. His tongue wound a path of wetness as his fingers kneaded my breasts, threading their way to my taut nipples. "What you did to me," he whispered.

Alyze's words came back to me. "I didn't mark you. I didn't bite you."

His lips broke from my neck, but his fingers worked my sensitive nipples. "We marked each other."

Holy freezing water submersion mood switch. "We? There is no we. I didn't do anything."

His hands dropped from my breasts and rested on my hips. In a way it was even more distracting, because every part of my body anticipated where they'd go next, and they all wanted a go with him. The horny little whores.

"We did, or at least our inner beasts did, whether we intended to or not." His hands slid down toward my thighs.

I clamped my hands on his, and his eyes widened as if he didn't realize what his appendages were doing.

"You might have an inner beast, but I don't. I'm a vampire. A Sempiternal pureblood."

He cocked his head. "You sure about that?"

"Yes. My mom and dad were Sempiternals. Top members of Silver Dagger Sisterhood and Silver Cloak Brotherhood, respectively."

He dipped his chin toward my exposed breasts, full-on tits hard as rocks. I crossed my arms over my chest. "Do you mind? I'm trying to have a heated conversation."

"I know parts you like heated," he purred in a deep voice reminiscent of his sex growls.

"Whoa," I said, backing away from him, fighting with something inside me that wanted to get heated all over again, and again, and again.

He leaned toward me, his gold eyes riming with red. Freaky flexible bastard.

"Stop. I want to talk to Jace," I grunted, still fighting with something in me.

"I am Jace. Every part of me." His guttural voice stirred my inner beast.

Oh goddess, I *did* have an inner beast.

"I want Jace."

"I know you do. Every part of you."

Oh gods, I strained to resist Jace's beast. There was only one word, however, that would stop him. One word I loathed to use except in extreme extenuating circumstances lest it lose its potency.

"No," I roared, battling both my inner beast and Jace's as I leapt away from him, covering my lady bits with his torn shirt. When had that happened? Was it me, Jace, or our inner beasts?

A magickal barrier separated us. Jace blinked a few times, the red disappearing from his eyes. "What happened?"

"Mr. Inner Beasty wanted to get frisky again. I pulled the 'No' card with him and mine."

He cursed. He held up his hands. "He's never taken control like that before." His gold eyes met mine. "He really wants you."

"Only him?" I prowled toward him.

A deep rumble vibrated from his chest. He pinched his lips together, his forehead wrinkling with the effort, but it wasn't enough. He wanted me, and I wanted him, and that was all there was to it. The magickal barrier between us wavered as my resolve wavered.

"*Resisto*," he shouted.

A blue translucent shield shot between us, knocking me flat on my ass. I shook my head, snapping out of whatever daze had just come over me. "What was that?"

"You mean who. Who was that? Your inner beast wants mine too."

I pressed my hands to my heart, trying to calm the thundering heartbeats and raging hormones. She had never come out before.

He raised an eyebrow—a very sexy eyebrow—and the thundering started all over again. I squeezed my skull, trying to fight her. "I can't tell my thoughts from hers."

"You and she are mostly the same, but you must learn to control her."

My eyes pierced through the blue shield. "Like you controlled yours?"

He nodded. "Point taken. I told you, that's never happened before."

I crossed my arms over my chest, my legs still bare, along with the rest of my lower half. He swallowed, trying not to look down. My anger returned. "Do you use that on all your students?"

His skin paled. "I'm twenty-five and this is my first assignment. Don't soil what exists between us with something tainted and dirty."

"What do we have between us other than two inner beasts horny as fuck?" My eyes dropped to his naked body and his sizeable cock returning to life. "And speaking of horny . . ." I swallowed roughly, trying to maintain control, "do you mind dressing?"

He squatted down to grab his pants, his leg muscles bulging with strength. His lips tipped into a small grin when he realized I was still watching him as he tugged on his pants. "Our inner beasts aren't the only ones who want each other."

All my lady bits sang, *yes, yes, YES!*

I rolled my eyes. "No, they aren't, but who and what is my inner beast, and how do I control her?"

"I could teach . . ." he started but didn't finish.

"Right. Because then we'd only learn how many orgasms we can have in two hours."

He squinted as if thinking, before his delicious dimple popped out, begging me to lick it. "At least seven, if I remember correctly."

"A lucky number."

"A very lucky number."

I could feel the pull of the universe drawing us together, but his shield stopped us. "So, who teaches me to control her?"

His forehead furrowed. "I might know someone."

"What do we do in the meantime about this whole marking thing? Is it permanent?"

His entire being drooped. "Don't you want it to be?"

I heard the longing in his voice. He wanted this. As much as he had tried to stay away from me for all those weeks, he wanted me as much as I wanted him. But the thing was, I couldn't tell which parts of my desire were mine and which belonged to my inner beast. I wanted to hunt monsters and kiss things. Things plural. Not just one thing.

But what a fine thing he is . . . She-Beasty murmured.

I took in Jace's sculpted bare chest and long, lean legs. His hands were propped behind his head, his muscular arms flexing as if he was trying to act casual but also resisting any temptation my presence caused.

"No, I don't want it to be permanent," I growled and stomped out of the room, only partially dressed.

Liar, She-Beasty growled.

TWENTY-SIX

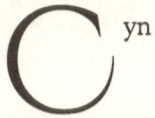yn

I CAUGHT up to Dez a few hours later prowling back to our room with no pants on and a ripped shirt that barely covered her butt cheeks.

"You had sex again."

"No, I like walking around with ass and pussy on display."

I gasped at her words. Dez commanded her body like a weapon. Her vocabulary reflected that. I'd never be as comfortable with my body as she was with hers.

"Yes, I had sex again," she sighed. "Long story, and I don't feel like talking about it right now. Have you seen Alyze? I've got to talk to her."

"No, but I think she and Anastasia were going to study out in the courtyard this afternoon."

She took off toward the courtyard door.

"Aren't you going to put pants on?"

She glanced down at her bare legs. "Oh yeah. Don't want to cause a sex riot or anything." She stopped, scratching her collarbone. "Although, that might get my mind off things."

Again with the sex-for-all vibes. She had no restraint whatsoever.

"Dez, are you at least on birth control? And you should use a condom. Birth control doesn't prevent sexually trans-mitted diseases."

"What is this, Junior High School Sex Talk 101? Yes, I'm on birth control, and yes, I use condoms." She paused and cleared her throat. "In most cases."

"Dez . . ."

She threw up her hand. "Don't give me a lecture. I've got more than unprotected sex on my mind."

I stepped closer so we weren't overheard. "Did you ask Jace about Canyon and the spell?"

She veered away from the outside door and took off down the hall toward our room.

I followed after her. "Did you?"

"No. Things got heated between us."

"I bet."

She side-eyed me with her trademark saucy grin. "There's hope for you yet, and you're right. After that heat, we argued. Again, long story, but no, I didn't ask him about Canyon." She stopped when we got to our room and looked at me. "Can I ask you something?"

"You're asking permission? That's not like you."

She leaned in, dipping her head toward my ear. "Have you ever felt anything or anyone inside you?"

I pulled away from her. "What do you mean?"

She pursed her lips and stormed into our room. "Nothing. Forget I said anything."

I followed her in, closing the door behind me. I hurried over to her, careful to keep my voice down. "Dez, what do you mean?"

Her mouth opened, but nothing came out.

I grabbed her arms and spun her to face me. "Dez, you're kinda freaking me out. It's not like you not to voice your mind. Just spit it out."

She breathed in and out. "Jace said I have an inner beast."

By the concerned tone of her voice, I figured she wasn't referring to her sex drive. "What kind of inner beast?"

"I don't know. We're supposed to be pureblood Sempiternals, but Jace said I have something else. So if I do, you do."

My sister was smart, but she overlooked the obvious. "Not definitely. Not if my biological father wasn't your biological father."

She knocked my hands aside. "We share the same mother and father. I know that for a fact," she snarled and slammed the bathroom door behind her.

I knocked on the door. "Dez, we need to talk about this."

"No, we don't. I need to shower."

"Can it wait? This is important."

"No, it can't." The bathroom fan grumbled to life as the shower started.

I rested against the door. What did Dez mean by 'inner beast'? She insisted we shared the same parents, but what if we didn't? The only way to prove it was a DNA test, ideally with blood, but Dez was so stubborn she'd never go for it.

My eyes fell on her hairbrush. Hair could work too. Well, not hair per se, but hair follicle root—and with the magickal capabilities here at Silverwood, I should be able to deduce if we shared enough DNA to be full siblings. Fifty percent or so would make us full siblings. Twenty-five percent or less would make us half siblings. I pulled all the strands out, clutched them in my hand, and hurried to the potions lab. Canyon was working this afternoon. I was supposed to stay away from him until we figured out what was going on. Technically, I was supposed to stay away from him period, but this DNA mystery seemed a lot more pressing.

I rushed over to the lab, excited to run my little experiment. Of course, I couldn't take Potion Making this semester since it leant to my strengths, but during the campus tour Canyon had given me, he'd mentioned the lab was open to all students. Since then, I'd taken to working on potions in my spare time. Science was my jam, and potion making rocked my world. Nothing like brewing up a concoction for acne or a lovely facial cream. Even Dez was using my products. She assumed I bought them from a Potions student, but again, what she didn't know wouldn't hurt her.

Much of potion making was about setting intention and establishing the proper procedures in order to successfully create a specific potion. Often students ran their own experiments, but they concentrated on love spells. Elementary at best. And they often backfired because dismissing another person's free will was the equivalent of revoking their consent. In other words, it violated Silverwood Academy rules. Not that I hadn't broken a few of my own, but after Rhiannon's visit, I'd locked that bloodlust back up.

I hurried into the lab and ran smack into Canyon. He

stumbled backward, nearly tipping over a small cauldron. He righted it just before any liquid spilled out.

"Sorry." I winced, my cheeks crimson, and not because I'd knocked into him. That last time we were together, I had almost sucked him dry. Dez assured me that she had compelled him to forget everything, but what if it didn't take? What if he remembered?

He frowned at me.

Yep, he definitely remembered.

"Cynda, you of all people should know better than to rush into the potions lab. It's dangerous for the potion creator, the unsuspecting assailant, and anyone in close proximity."

Of course I knew better. I was a scientist. But I couldn't help smiling anyway. He didn't remember anything from last night. "You're right. I apologize. It won't happen again."

His green eyes sparkled as his face brightened. Something inside me began vibrating with need and desire. I swallowed hard.

"Good. I should hope so. Hey, sorry I bailed on our study session last night. I blanked on it and passed out by eight." He scratched at the side of his head as if he was trying to remember what had really happened but couldn't quite catch it. "It's unlike me, but you know . . . life."

Well done, Dez. Well done.

I turned from him and headed in the direction of the cauldron cabinet, trying to act as indifferent as possible while fighting the thing inside me. "No problem. I went to bed early too."

I could just imagine my sister saying, "I bet you did."

I ran my fingers over the different sizes of cauldrons. A size 3 or 4 was too small. A 15 or 20—much too big. A 7

195

should do it. I pulled it out and spun around, slamming into a firm, muscular chest.

Why hellooo, sexy . . .

I stilled. What in the name of the Goddess was that?

Don't you mean 'who'?

I closed my eyes, trying to quiet the new voice in my head. What was happening to me? Last night I'd returned from Rhiannon feeling calm and confident. Now my world was tipping sideways. Again. I squinted hard, as if I could repair whatever shorted connection existed inside my brain that could cause these feelings.

"Cynda?" I heard someone say, but I was too focused on quieting my mind. That's what Professor Bladecroft had taught us. Quiet your mind before taking action.

Two strong hands gripped my shoulders. "Cynda, are you okay?"

I opened my eyes to Canyon standing much too close, his concerned blue eyes watching me. Red circled his irises. His lips were mere inches from my own. His musky, earthy scent flooded my nose, and my inner beast stirred.

Shit. I had an inner beast too.

Canyon's nostrils flared in and out, as if catching my change of mood, which didn't make any sense because he was an ephemeral, a human. Though Dez's question to him came rushing back to me. *What are you, Canyon?* she had asked, as if he was something other than human. But he hadn't answered her, or not that I'd heard anyway, and I wasn't about to ask him now. I didn't want to compel him or anyone else. Plus, I didn't know how. I had to get out of there.

"Bite me, Cyn," he growled, opening his neck to me. His carotid artery pulsed with desire, begging me to take a bite. Just one taste. Just—

"No," I shouted. I pushed him away and dashed out of the lab. My chest heaved and my blood thrummed. My body throbbed with need. I vamp-sped down the hall to cries of "Cynda!" following me long after I was out of sight. I pushed through the nearest door and dashed outside. Cold, clean air brushed over my face, clearing my senses and mind of Canyon's seductive scent. I collapsed against the nearest oak tree to help stabilize and ground myself. The rough bark brought me to the present.

Let's go back, the voice inside my head purred.

Who are you, and why are you here? I thought.

I'm you. Well, a part of you.

And what is that?

Can you keep a secret?

My stomach curled in dread. Secrets often led to dark paths I didn't want to travel.

When I didn't answer, she continued. *We've met before.*

I stiffened. What was she talking about? *I think I'd remember that.*

First few days of Silverwood Prison were kinda hazy, weren't they?

Yes, they were, but that was because I had just died.

You mean you had Awakened.

Dez killed me so I'd turn early, so I died.

You are Awake now, and every full moon from now on.

Full moon? As in . . .

One plus one half plus one half equals . . . she teased in a singsong voice not unlike a song I remembered from my early childhood. But I was in no mood for riddles or games.

Do the math for me.

One pure Semipiternal plus one not-so-pure Semipiternal equals one Semipiternal wolf shifter.

My hackles rose—no pun intended. *I'm a wolf shifter?*

And a born vampire. So is your sister.

Crap. *When's the next full moon?*

Any guesses? she sang.

I slammed a barrier down in my mind and rushed off to find Deziree, my fingers curling into fists, my nails digging into my palms. This had better not be one of the secrets she was hiding. And if it wasn't, well, she'd find out soon enough.

CHAPTER
TWENTY-SEVEN

D^{ez}

DRESSED and showered for the second time today, I rushed out of my room in hopes of finding Alyze and Red in the courtyard. I trusted them with my life. I skidded to a stop, the realization blowing my mind. Growing up, I didn't have many friends. Any, in fact. Moving around all the time with a father who hunted monsters for a living made for difficult first conversations, and the lies eventually caught up to me. That, and I really was a bitch.

Of course, the no-friends thing was one of the reasons I turned Cynda. I wanted someone in my life. Alyze and Anastasia had weaseled their way into my heart too. I never thought I could trust anyone outside my blood family, but everything inside me told me I could trust them. Let's pray my instincts were right, because with what was going on inside my body and the whole Jace-marking thing, our friendship would be tested.

The two of them were huddled under the very oak tree Jace had pushed me up against the night after the Induction Ceremony. My body thrummed with need. My goddess, I couldn't even think of him without everything south of my belly button getting in on the action. I pushed the horniness aside and hurried over.

I folded my legs and sat on the ground across from them. "Whatsup, ladies?"

They both grinned at me. "Dez, we were just talking about you."

I narrowed my eyes at Alyze, feeling the stab of betrayal. Maybe our friendship wasn't as strong as I thought it was, because I had specifically told her to keep her mouth shut about the marking thing. Compelled her, in fact. "You were?"

She nodded, the corner of her lip raising. "Yes, we need your opinion on what magickal ability you'd rather have. Flying or telepathy."

I frowned at her. Did she think I was an idiot? "Flying or telepathy? Seriously?"

"Yes," Red said. "Don't give Alyze that evil eye. Whatever secrets you shared with her are still a secret. Well, until now. Talk."

Red got right to the heart of the matter. I liked that about her.

"First, probably flying, because it seems to be the only magickal ability I don't have a chance of acquiring."

Red tilted her head. "So, you can read our minds?"

"Well, not your minds yet, but . . ." I sighed running my fingers through my hair, much like Jace had done during our heated conversation.

It was heated all right.

I needed to stop using that word, because my horny she-beast might erupt.

Alyze reached out and touched my knee. A zap of electricity shot through me, snapping me back to the present. "Dez, you with us?"

"It's complicated." My eyes shot from Alyze to Red then back to Alyze.

"You know you can trust Anastasia too, right?"

Red glared at me. "You don't trust me?"

I slapped my hands against my knees. "That's the crazy thing. I do. I totally do."

"And why is that crazy?"

"Long, complicated story, and not important." I glanced over both my shoulders, ensuring we were alone before continuing. "Alyze told me I was marked."

Red glanced at Alyze. "You caught that scent too?"

Alyze nodded. "I did."

"You can smell it too? Do I stink? I just showered again."

Alyze grinned. "Ah, that's why it smells fresh. He marked you a second time."

I looked over both my shoulders again. "Can everyone smell it?"

They both shook their heads. "No."

"Well, that answer's as clear as fuck."

"Oh, honey," Red said, "you fucked all right. I am one of Brigit's children, so I identify closely with Fire. Your aura burns extra bright now, and it smells liked smoked heat."

"And Morrigan is my primary goddess. Water is my closest element with Earth as my second. To me, your internal energy ripples off you in intense waves. You smell like fresh dew on a grassy meadow."

I breathed in and out through my nose. "So let me get

this straight. I look and smell like different things to each of you. Again I ask, can everyone else tell? Do I look and smell different to them?"

They glanced at each other, scrunching up their faces as if they were having an internal conversation. Maybe they were telepathic.

"I don't think so," Red finally said.

I cursed, not liking her answer one bit.

Alyze raised her hand, somehow calming me. "We're both really in tune with our goddess and our element and really in tune with you. You know that the others in our class aren't as advanced as the four of us, right?"

"Four as in me, you, Red, and . . ."

Her head tilted upward. "Cyn. Hey, Cyn, sit down. We were just talking about you too."

I glanced up in surprise that my sister had appeared as if out of thin air. She quickly folded down next to me, the whites of her eyes as wild as her hair, her blood racing through her veins.

"What's wrong?"

"What's wrong? What's wrong?" she asked, her voice rising by the second. "I'll tell you what's wrong. I almost bit him again."

"Who?" Alyze asked.

Cyn looked over both of her shoulders. She was as paranoid as I was. She leaned in and whispered. "Canyon."

"Again, as in you did already?" Alyze asked quietly.

Cyn bit her lip, nodding.

Red held a single finger to her mouth. "Hold on." She lifted both hands into the air and chanted a few lines. I recognized some of the words and realized it was a silencing spell. A shimmer of magick glided over us. "We can all speak freely now. No one can even see us."

"You really are powerful, aren't you?" I'd met a lot of witches through the years, and only a handful could muster up a silencing invisibility cloak fully enclosing four people.

"I told you."

"You did. Trust thing, remember?"

"I remember," she grinned. "But you can trust us. We aren't in the Sisterhood yet, but we will be . . ." She spun a raised circle in the air including each of us. "All four of us will be."

It was convenient to have a seer within your friend group. Heck, it was a novelty to have a friend group.

Alyze beamed proudly. It was convenient to have a siren in the friend group too. I hoped Cyn and I proved as worthy.

I leaned toward my sister, as drawn to her now as I had been when I first met her. "So, you almost bit Canyon again? I told you to stay away from him. What happened?"

She swallowed hard, glancing over at me. "Promise you won't be mad . . ."

I didn't like where this conversation was headed. I crossed my arms. "No promises, but I'll try."

"You'll do better than try," Alyze said, her words numbing my body.

I squinted at her, aware she had cast magick over me. "I didn't give you permission."

She waved her hand. "What happens in the circle, stays in the circle."

I rolled my eyes. Of course every single one of my friends was a rabble-rousing pain in the ass, and I loved them for it. "Fine. Cyn, just know that if you say—" My throat went numb, and words stopped coming out of my mouth—and it burned like a holy mother. I jerked my hands to my throat. "What did you do to me, Alyze?"

She shrugged. "If you can't say anything nice, you can't say anything at all."

Ouch. That spell was going to hurt. "Okay, go ahead, dearest sister."

Cyn licked her lips. "So, last night—well, super early this morning—Dez and I were talking about . . ." she glanced over at me as if unsure whether she should continue with the topic of our conversation. Jace said I shouldn't trust anyone, but he didn't appreciate the strength and power of sisterhood. I nodded to her. "We were talking about our dealings with Goddess Lilith and my meeting Goddess Rhiannon."

If they were shocked by this admission of our goddess meetings, they didn't show it. Quite the opposite, in fact.

Red lifted out of her cross-legged position, barely able to contain herself. "Is Lilith as cool as the stories make her out to be?"

I snapped my fingers. "Most definitely and more so."

"I knew it." She settled back into her seated position, content with the new knowledge.

Alyze rubbed her hands together. "And Rhiannon, what was she like? As elusive as the stories claim?"

"Yes," Cyn replied. "She remains to most a mystery, but she is always there."

"Wow," Alyze sighed. "Amazing."

"She really is, but Jace told Dez not to tell anyone about our dealings with the different goddesses."

They both pressed their lips together as if they didn't agree with him. When they didn't answer right away, my shoulders tensed, and I found it hard to breathe. Shit, maybe I shouldn't have trusted Jace. Maybe my instincts were wrong.

Finally Red said, "That's wise advice."

"It is," Alyze confirmed.

An invisible weight lifted. "Jace told me Cyn and I needed to stay away from Professor Goldwell."

Alyze frowned. "The Ghostbusting professor?"

I nodded.

"Why?"

"I don't know. Our second night here, I ran into him in the hallway."

"I bet you did." Alyze winked at me.

"Professor Goldwell showed up and took a sudden interest in me. Then Lilith appeared, and she was pissed at Goldwell. She sent Jace and me away."

"What did Goldwell do when Lilith showed up?"

"She kinda freaked, which I didn't fully appreciate because, like I said, Cyn and I had hung out with Lilith, so I didn't think her appearance was that big of a deal." Everyone nodded as if they understood my reaction. Whew! I didn't realize I needed their reassurance as much as I did. "That's when Jace rushed me outside, pushed me up against this tree, and—"

Cynda swung up her hand to stop me. "Whoa, whoa, whoa. We don't want to hear about your sexcapades."

"Speak for yourself," both Alyze and Red said together.

"We didn't have sex then, but it was hot as hell. He leaned in close to keep our conversation between us. That's when he told me to stay away from Goldwell and not tell anyone about our meetings with Lilith."

Red scratched her knee. "Did he say why?"

"No."

Alyze's forehead bunched. "And you trust him? The person who doesn't trust easily."

My insides thrummed in agreement. "I do."

"But he marked you."

205

Cyn swooped up my hair, searching my neck and collar-bone. "Marked? Where? What does that mean?"

I breathed in and out, grounding myself, because I could feel myself coming undone. Especially since I didn't understand it myself. "We marked each other."

Red, a child of Brigit, a fiercely independent woman, scrunched her face up in disgust. It matched Alyze's reaction. "You did? Purposely?"

"No, not on purpose. Jace thinks our inner beasts did."

"Inner beast?" Alyze asked. "I thought you were pure Sempiternal."

"I did too. That's what Dad told me, but She-Beasty came out when I confronted Jace, and the only way I got her away from him was to pull the 'No' card. That spell's freaking powerful."

Cyn smacked my knee. "That's what I did with Canyon when he tempted me to bite him again!"

"Why did you go to him after what happened last night?"

"He works at the potions lab, and I wanted to run a DNA test."

Anger bloomed in me. I had a sinking suspicion I knew what she wanted to find out. "DNA? On what?"

She pulled out a handful of hair.

"Ew, is that mine? Are you walking around with my hair in your pocket? What's wrong with you?"

She pushed the clump back inside her pants. "Nothing's wrong with me. I wanted to test the theory that maybe we didn't share the same parents."

A growl rippled from my chest. "We do. I told you we do."

"Yes, but you're taking Dad's word. I wanted irrefutable proof, and I didn't think you'd agree to a blood test, so I . . ."

"Took my hair."

She nodded. "I went to the lab and ran into Canyon, and that's where things took a turn."

"I bet," Red added, waggling her eyebrows.

"Did you get to run the test?" Alyze asked, surprisingly not jumping on the sexual innuendo train.

"No, and I don't need to. I met *my* inner beast."

My jaw unhinged from my skull. "You met her?"

"I did. She's my wolf. She said we were wolf shifters too."

"Whoa," Red said, flinging out her arms. Power waved off of them, snapping our mouths shut. "You're vampires and wolf shifters? Is that even possible?"

Cyn rubbed her hand across her collarbones, as if trying to keep her she-beast inside her. "Evidently, it is."

"So you're some kind of hybrid."

Cyn shrugged, not realizing the implications of Alyze's statement. "I guess so."

Red rubbed her temples. "But you're Sempiternals. Born vampires."

I lifted my chest, needing to defend my heritage. "We are."

"But you're wolf shifters too?"

"I guess so." The truth of my words thrummed through me.

Alyze's head bopped up and down. "That's why you and Jace marked each other. It's a shifter thing. Is he a wolf?"

"I don't know."

But if he wasn't a wolf, what was he?

207

TWENTY-EIGHT

yn

THE FOUR OF us came up with a plan. Tag line: Keep it cool. Dez and I would stay away from Canyon and Jace, and Alyze and Red would make a special potion to prevent Dez and me from turning into wolves at the full moon, which happened to be tonight.

Easy-peasy, right?

Wrong.

"What's taking them so long?" Dez hissed, circling our bedroom for the fiftieth time. Good thing we didn't have a rug, because she'd have worn a path already.

I glanced up from my journal, pretending to be relaxed and not the least bit worried. A lie, of course. "They'll be here."

"What are you writing about anyway?" She peered over my shoulder before I could cover the page with my elbow.

"Driving down the steep three-mile hill into the valley was the only memory I could call up. That and the crazy look in my sister's eye."

She huffed. "It wasn't crazy. It was excitement. I couldn't wait for you to become a vampire and join Silverwood Academy with me."

I rolled my eyes, annoyed at her invasion of privacy. "Come on, Dez. Can't I have one thing that doesn't include you? One thing that's just mine?"

She returned to her pacing. "Canyon. You can have Canyon. Actually, no. You can't have him. He's Goldwell's son. He can't be trusted."

"Last night—did Jace ever tell you what supernatural being he was?"

She squinted at me. "Guess I can't have privacy either."

"Not when it involves someone I care about."

She threw her hands in the air, circling around again. "You barely know him."

"And you barely know Jace."

She stopped and stared at me. "Jace is different."

My inner beast snarled. I stood, flaring out my chest, ready to fight. "Why? Because you know better than me?"

She appeared inches from me, her chest flared out as well. "I *do* know better than you. I've lived a supernatural life, remember? I grew up with Dad, a Sempiternal, a member of Silver Cloak Brotherhood. I know this life. You know nothing."

"I know more than you think." My she-wolf clawed at my insides to get out.

Dez's purple eyes flashed brightly, her wolf rising to the challenge. "I doubt that, little sister."

"Anytime, big sister," I growled in a voice I didn't recognize.

Her eyes flashed again. My eyes fell to her arms where fur sprouted. Rage swirled inside me. If that was how she was going to play it . . .

Our bedroom door burst open, slamming into the wall. Jace shoved himself between us, his wide shoulders pushing me back. "Submit," he roared.

The fight inside me was immediately extinguished, as though I'd been shoved into an icy cold shower. I blinked a few times before meeting Dez's eyes. The fur was gone from her arms, and her eyes had returned to normal.

She held her head with her hands. "What was that?"

"That," a woman said, stalking into the room and closing the door behind her, "was your wolves trying to surface."

She wore an elegant, classically styled, long midnight-blue dress. She felt familiar, like a part of me trying to surface.

"You're Goddess Morrigan," I whispered.

She winked at me. "You're at least familiar with me. Good. That'll make this conversation a lot easier." Her attention shifted to Jace, who stood staring at her with his mouth open. "You can go. I'll take care of them." He shifted, as if about to protest, then nodded and disappeared out the door.

Dez kept blinking, as if she couldn't believe her eyes. She didn't say a word, which wasn't like her. Her throat bobbed as she swallowed a few times, trying to find her voice. Then, finally, she said, "Mom?"

My head whipped back and forth between the two. Panic crept its way up my spine and grabbed hold of my throat. "Mom? What do you mean 'Mom'?" I choked out before my breath was ripped from me.

Morrigan snapped her fingers and her gorgeous dress

disappeared, replaced by a midnight-blue tank top with the water emblem and matching jeans. Even her combat boots were midnight blue. She clasped her hands behind her back and stretched. "Aw, that's better. I wanted to appear to you both as a goddess should for our reunion, but that's not really my cup of tea, aside from the fact I prefer dry red."

I stood watching her. Her resemblance to Dez was uncanny. There was no disputing where my sister got her purple eyes from.

"I thought you were dead," Dez said through clenched teeth, blinking hard, but this time it was to fight back the tears threatening to spill over.

Morrigan blinked several times as well, trying to stop her own tears. "It was easier that way."

"Easier for who? You? You didn't want the responsibility of raising two daughters?"

Morrigan opened her mouth, then closed it again. She pressed her lips together, either because she didn't know what to say or she didn't want to say the wrong thing.

Dez slammed her hand on her hip, grabbing hold of her rage like an old friend. "Well?"

Morrigan looked at me, then Dez, then to the beds and chair. "We should sit. This conversation will take a while."

My sister crossed her arms over her chest. "I'll stand, thanks."

Morrigan's nostrils flared. She might be our mom, but she was a goddess too and expected—no, demanded—respect. "Fine. Have it your way." She snapped her fingers again. A bright light exploded, blinding me, and suddenly, we were no longer standing in our room. We were in an enormous grove that smelled divine. Blossoms exploded like fireworks across the trees. I studied the flowers and leaves, trying to place them. Nothing like compartmental-izing our current situation through distraction.

"It's an apple grove. The apple bough is my symbol of peace and plenty."

Dez stood with her hands fisted at her sides. "You need a shit-ton more apple orchards to make up for your vanishing act. Why did Dad lie? He told me you were a top member of Silver Dagger Sisterhood."

"I *am* a top member. One of the five."

Dez growled. "That's not what I meant. He said you gorged yourself on blood after Cynda's birth and disap-peared. He was always very clear about what happens to rogue vampires who can't control their bloodlust."

Three ravens landed in the grove with us. The birds were a symbol of Goddess Morrigan, who evidently was my mom.

I rubbed my temples. This night, like many nights since I'd entered this supernatural world, overloaded me with too many thoughts, too many out-of-this-world elements to process, too many of everything. "I can't . . ." I paced around in a tight circle, the ravens enclosing us with their freaking huge bodies, and freaking huge wings, and freaking huge beaks. "I can't . . ."

"Can't what, Cynda?" Morrigan asked, sounding almost motherly.

"You don't get to call her that," Dez barked, sounding more wolf than sister.

Morrigan lifted her chin. "Why not? I'm the one who named her. I'm the one who named both of you. Of course, my sisters helped, suggesting names equating to that which spoke to every man's most base needs, Cyn and Dezire. Get it? Your names serving as an attack against those that herald male-based religions instead of recognizing that there are men and women gods."

Dez scowled at her, but the words that came out of her mouth next surprised me. I had assumed she'd go for the jugular—that was her usual MO, but she didn't seem bothered that our names symbolized man's weakness. Oh no, she didn't seem shocked by that at all. "Your sisters, as in . . ."

Morrigan's eyes brightened. "The five of us, of course. Maeve, Lilith, Rhiannon, Brigit, and me. The five who, with the guidance of our mother, Mother Earth, Anu, Gaia, whatever your preference is, created Silver Dagger Sisterhood."

Dez slammed her fist into her hand. Energetic power flew off it like shooting stars in the night sky. "So they knew you were our mom and said nothing? Lilith didn't think to mention it at our induction or any time after?" She aimed her fingers at me. "Rhiannon didn't find it appropriate to share with Cyn the other night when she revealed herself to her? Left the mark of the goddess on her?"

Now that she put it that way, she made a point. They'd all had a chance to tell us but didn't. But then I remembered Jace's warning to Dez, and some of the pieces fell into place. "That's the reason Dez and I aren't supposed to share with anyone that we've seen and talked with the goddesses."

Morrigan pressed her lips together. "Yes."

Dez's purple eyes widened, then she pinched her lips together as if realizing something else. She stared at our mom. "Goldwell is after us because of you, isn't she?"

Morrigan shifted her feet as if confronting an uncomfortable truth. The action almost made her seem human.

"Goldwell suspects I am your mother."

"And why is that a problem?"

Morrigan's purple eyes, so much like my sister's, fell on her, then me, as she breathed in and out, considering her next words. "There are several reasons."

Dez clapped her hands together. "I've got all night."

A wave of dizziness overtook me. My knees buckled, and I collapsed to the ground. "Actually, I don't think we do."

My wolf quivered. *It's almost time.*

"No, it's not," Morrigan yelled. She rubbed her hands together, murmuring something. Two bright blue fireballs burst forth, pushing her palms apart. "I'm sorry, girls, but this conversation must be delayed until another day."

"Figures," Dez snarled from a long snout with large canines lengthening by the very second as she, too, dropped to the ground on all fours.

We have to get away from her, my wolf pleaded with me.

"I really am sorry," Morrigan cried as she hurled the fireballs at us.

Screams ripped from my lungs, spiraling into the air, combining with Dez's screams. White hot pain tore through me until blackness fell.

Your inner beast will not surface for many moons. It is not time for her yet. You can never share with anyone that I am your mother, but believe me, Cynda, I am. I love you and will do all I can to protect you, but there are forces outside of my realm of influence I can't fight. Stay safe. Dez will protect you.

CHAPTER
TWENTY-NINE

ez

YOUR INNER BEAST will not surface for many moons. Her presence is not yet needed. Do not share my identity with anyone. I love you and will do all I can to protect you, but you well know there are forces outside of my realm of influence. Dez, continue your training. You are a warrior. Protect your sister.

THE WORDS OF MY MOTHER, Morrigan, The Morrigan, as many called her, whispered in and out of my subconscious until they finally wiggled their way into my brain.

It had been a long time since I heard my mother's voice. Almost two decades, in fact. That truth hurt more than I cared to admit. I was four when our mother abandoned us. Four, when my sister was ripped from me. Four, when my family unit ceased to exist, and my dad became all I had.

215

Was I bitter? Yes.

Was I angry with my mother? Yes.

Would I listen to her warning? Also yes.

I knew enough about this world that not listening to her would be akin to hammering a silver stake into my own heart. No one could know who our mother was, but it did explain how we could be pure Sempiternals but also wolf shifters. As Queen of Shapeshifters, she established the rules for all shifters, and how to break said rules. The question was, why did she want to keep our wolves hidden? Wouldn't it be better to release them while at Silverwood Academy so we could at least learn how to control them and the primal instincts that came with them?

I leapt up from my bed. The deep sleep of last night angered me now that I was fully awake. It wasn't natural rest. It was a side effect of whatever spell Mommy Dearest had shot at us to prevent us from turning into our wolves.

"I see you slept well," Cyn said from her bed, the snarky remark making my lip curl into a half smile. "Do you want to talk about what happened?"

And pop goes the smile. "No," I said, rushing over to her bed. "And neither do you. We can't talk about it."

"But . . ." she tried.

"No. I was there. You were there. No need to discuss. No need to rehash. No need to ever talk about it again."

"I beg to differ."

"Of course you do." I punched my hands into her mattress, trapping her under her comforter. Her light green eyes widened. The flecks of purple in them reminded me of Mom. "Listen, we don't tell anyone about this. Not Anastasia, not Alyze, not Jace, and definitely not Canyon."

She thrashed against my hold, trying to unseat me. I

pushed harder with the grim satisfaction that my sister really had no idea how strong I was. No one here did.

"But they know about our wolves."

"They do, but they don't know about our parentage, and they can never know."

"Won't they suspect it? Jace made us submit to him for goddess's sake."

My lips pressed in a thin line. "It's not common. Less common than our hybrid status."

She gasped, realizing the weight of my words. "Really? I mean, I read *Percy Jackson*. There was an entire camp dedicated to half-bloods."

I rolled my eyes. My sister had to go there. "That's Greek and Roman mythology *and* fiction. Our situation is real life, and I'm telling you, it's rare. Like unheard of."

She collapsed back into the bed, no longer resisting me. "Really?"

"Really. Now, get your ass up and let's get on with our day, pretending we were the exact same people we were yesterday. Got it?" I glared at her with my evil eye, which was quite intimidating.

Her chest huffed as she released her breath. "Got it."

I slowly lifted my hands as I watched her for any sudden movements or surprise attacks. Finally free, she pushed herself into a seated position and looked at me.

"Why didn't you tell me who she was?"

"I didn't know."

She frowned, raising an eyebrow. "You didn't suspect it?"

"No."

"Not even a little? You had to have studied the . . ." She glanced over each of her shoulders as if someone was listening. She cleared her throat, not wanting to take a chance. "Them. You had to have studied them."

The thing was, I had studied them. Dad had made me honor each goddess every night. I knew each of them equally well, but he never hinted he'd had a relationship with one. He held them all equally in his heart, which, given our present circumstances, was cause for concern. Women could have multiple children, but they carried every baby in their womb. A guy, however, could spread his seeds like spring planting season.

"What?"

I snapped back to reality. "Nothing."

Dad would have told me if I had other sisters. He only ever talked about Cyn. He cared deeply for his daughters—his two daughters—and he wouldn't have abandoned us if there was any other way. If there were forces at work outside of the goddesses' and gods' realm of influence, Cyn and I, along with the rest of the future Silver Dagger Sisterhood and Silver Cloak Brotherhood, had to be ready.

"Let's go eat. I'm starving."

WINDING up on my ass was not how I planned to spend my afternoon, but then again, after the last twenty-four hours, give or take, I really shouldn't have expected anything less.

Cyn snickered from her perch atop a gorgeous blue roan, which evidently described the mottled gray coat of the stallion she was riding.

I pushed myself off the ground and wiped away the grass and dirt from my fall. "How did you get the calm, well-behaved horse, and I got the hellion? You're the one with horse experience."

"We could switch," she offered, swinging her leg over and hopping to the ground. The horse nickered at her as she led it over to me and offered me the reins. I eyed the long pieces of leather as if they were two coiled snakes about to strike.

"Just hop on?" I asked, grabbing the reins.

"Well, put the reins back over his head, and then I'll give you a leg up to get into the saddle."

"Why? I didn't need to do that with Red Devil over there."

Red Devil, a.k.a. Miss Ruffles, was eating grass as if she hadn't just vaulted her rider off her back.

Cyn shook her head, watching me. "You really don't know anything about horses, do you?"

"No, and thanks for the reminder." How did you get in this class anyway, since you clearly know everything there is to know about them? Obviously, riding is a strength of yours."

She pursed her lips. "Horses aren't the only things we'll ride."

My prospects brightened tremendously. "I can't wait to get my sore rump on a Harley."

She shook her head. "Yeah, well, those things scare the crap out of me. I much prefer horses to any other mode of transportation."

"You're weird. You know that, right?"

"That's what you keep telling me. Now, are you going to get on Blue Rays or continue to keep stalling?" She squatted down and intertwined her fingers together next to Blue Rays for me to put my foot in.

"Why do I need a leg up again?"

She stood up. "See this saddle? It's an English saddle— remember my explanation the first day of class?"

I waved her off. "That was ages ago. I was preoccupied."

She sighed. "Yeah, well, Miss Ruffles has a Western saddle on. Thick stirrups, a horn, along with a thick, cushioned seat. The English saddle has no horn and a lot less leather, allowing the rider to use her legs more to steer the horse rather than rely on neck reining, which is required with Western saddles."

My eyes crossed as most of her words went in one ear and out the other. "You mean to tell me I don't have a horn to hold on to in case Old Blue takes off on me?"

He snorted as if he didn't like my nickname for him and that, yes, in fact, he did plan to take off on me.

I eyed him suspiciously. "He understands what I'm saying, doesn't he?"

She scratched his neck. "To some degree, yes, but it's more like he senses your apprehension, and Blue Rays is a stallion. Spunk is his middle name."

"It's my middle name too, but I don't want a horse with it. Is there another one I could use? Or maybe I'll walk back. It's been a *day* anyway."

She gathered the reins and took off with Old Blue toward Red Devil. "Come on, I'll help you get back on Miss Ruffles. She's much more your speed."

I followed after her. "My speed? She bucked me off."

She laughed, finding my pain funny. "She didn't buck you off. You didn't tighten the girth and you sorta slipped off."

"Thanks for telling me. Geez, I hate to see how you act with someone you don't like."

She grinned at me, the sun catching the streaks of purple in her light green eyes. "Who said I liked you?"

I grabbed Red Devil's reins and started walking. "Okay, okay. I've created a monster with an attitude."

"Yes, you have. But it's okay. I'm dealing."

I glanced over at her. She'd never admitted she liked her new life before.

She leaned toward me. "I mean, we have a mom, and she's freaking amazing."

I groaned. "You've been reading again, haven't you? What did I tell you about that nasty habit—it leads to ideas and opinions. Leave those to me."

She snorted, sounding exactly like Old Blue as she tightened Red Devil's girth. "I've seen you reading plenty of times. You just want to be the one who acts like you know everything and tells me what to do."

I patted her shoulder. "Finally we understand each other."

"We understand each other all right, and you're getting your ass back in the saddle."

"But ..."

She grabbed the reins from me and placed them over Red Devil's neck. "What happens when you fall off a horse?"

"You sprint to your room and never get on one again?"

"No, you get back on. Now, put your boot in the stirrup and giddyup."

Her jaw was set in a hard line, which I'd come to realize was her own brand of stubbornness. "Fine, but if I wind up on my ass again, I quit, and there ain't nothing you can do about it."

Her lips cracked into a smile. "Agreed. You won't fall. Trust Miss Ruffles like you trust me."

I squinted at her. "What makes you think I trust you."

"You do," she replied confidently before nodding her chin at the stirrup. "Now, get on."

I grabbed the reins, placed my boot in the stirrup,

swung my leg over Red Devil, and shoved my other boot into the other stirrup, almost as if I knew what I was doing.

"Now, wait for me."

She disappeared from my side and appeared on Blue Rays's back. I narrowed my eyes at her. "I thought you said, I needed a leg up to get on an English saddle."

She winked at me. "You do. I don't. Blue Rays trusts me, and I trust him."

"And I trust you," I confessed.

Her face brightened. "And I mostly trust you."

"That's fair."

She steered her horse alongside me and Red Devil. "Let's ride."

And we did.

THIRTY

C^{yn}

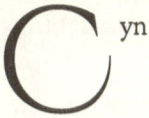

Landing on my ass was not the way I wanted to spend my morning. Dez had spent enough time on hers yesterday, and as I pushed myself up from the mat again, I supposed it was karma for laughing at her. I had never spared karma much thought, but it definitely was something to consider in this new supernatural world I lived in now. Three ravens circled overhead. I knew they were there for me. Morrigan's ravens had begun attending all our outside activities and exercises.

Dez had cursed at them yesterday and even threatened to throw sticks at them, but still, they circled and circled, watching and observing, taking notes to return to Mom Morrigan.

I still hadn't completely processed how I felt about meeting my actual birth mom, and her being alive, and that she was Goddess Morrigan, and that all her sisters were invested in our success. To what end, I didn't know, but I didn't want to spend too much time overthinking it, because my opponent, a dragon shifter named Ramone, wasn't taking it easy on me, and if I didn't step up and kick a little ass, Professor Bladecroft would ensure I spent the rest of my morning running around the track until I dropped from exhaustion. Last week's session had ended that way, and my muscles still ached from it.

"Get up," Ramone grunted. "I haven't even broken a sweat yet."

I brushed the dirt from my pants. At least leather pants were stretchy and didn't tear easily. No grass stains either.

"If it's any consolation, I broke a nail," I offered, lifting my broken fingernail to him.

"It's not. Why Bladecroft wanted me to train with you, I will never know. You're a joke of a warrior."

I smiled at him with my fangs fully extended. "Oh, you're such a charmer. Never let anyone tell you otherwise."

"Your teeth don't impress or intimidate me." He revealed a full set of dragon teeth.

"I'll remember that. Perhaps she wants me to teach you patience?"

"Patience is unnecessary in battle," he roared, sprinting toward me with his arms aimed right for my chest. No, he didn't care about the twins one bit, as evidenced by the same bull-headed approach he'd taken a minute ago. I breathed in and out, assessing the situation. He was strong and fast, but I was faster. I stepped to the side at the last second. He flew off the mat and landed face first in the grass.

"Well done, Cynda." Professor Bladecroft clapped as she

approached our mat. "You're finally incorporating the methods and techniques I've been teaching you."

"Avoidance? 'Cause I've mastered that one."

She grinned at me. "Avoidance is an evasion technique. In hand-to-hand combat, Ramone will pummel you."

"Appreciate the encouragement." Goddess, I was sounding more and more like my sister.

"But," she held up a single finger, "if you understand your strengths and weaknesses, along with your opponent's, you can and will best him every time. And patience is a necessary component of battle strategy, don't you agree, Ramone?"

He grunted, neither confirming nor denying her statement.

She spun around in a circle, clapping loudly to signal all the students to stop what they were doing and pay attention. She tapped her head. "Using your head will guide you on the battlefield and in life. Patience and," her gaze fell on me, "avoidance, are vital tools available to those willing to use them." She glanced down at Ramone's crumpled body. "Physical prowess will only get you so far." She raised a clenched fist into the air. "Mental aptitude will always be your greatest strength. Some have it," she circled around, her eyes falling on many of the students, including me, "and some don't. That is the purpose of Silverwood Academy—to prepare future Sisters and Brothers. But not all of you will make it. You might decide to leave today, tomorrow, or next week, or you will wait until the graduation and discover a new path awaits you outside of Silver Dagger Sisterhood or Silver Cloak Brotherhood."

Ramone groaned as he rose to his feet, swaying back and forth like a tree in a heavy wind, but unlike the tree with its deep, steadying roots, he looked as if he'd be knocked over by the slightest of breezes. I guess the old saying was true: The bigger they are, the harder they fall.

Indeed, a voice replied in my head, but it wasn't my inner wolf, who'd been quiet since Mom had shot us with that spell the other night. It wasn't Lilith or Rhiannon either.

Mom?

My Ravens shared that you felled a much larger opponent.

Did they also tell you I got my ass kicked prior to that fall?

The past forms your present. Your present develops your future. Perceived failures are but building blocks. I must go now, but well done.

Her voice faded from my head, and now that I was loosely aware of her presence there, I keenly felt her absence.

She'd better think twice about creeping in on Dez's mind, though. She'd find curses, scandalous thoughts, and vulgar language in that order.

"Come with me, Cynda. I'd like to speak with you. May I?" Professor Bladecroft asked as her hand hovered over my arm.

I snapped back to the present. Was it weird she wanted to touch my arm? I thought so, but I went with it anyway. "Sure?"

I only wish to communicate with you privately.

I stiffened. Here we go again. *You can read my thoughts?*

Only when I touch you. I'm a tactile telepathic.

Okay . . . I said carefully, not sure why she'd shared that information with me or how it affected me, because I already owned a closet full of secrets.

You did well today. You are finally beginning to tap into your abilities.

You already said that aloud. Why the secrecy now?

Because others may be listening.

The hairs on the back of my neck stood on end. *What do you mean?*

As your abilities grow, you need to start holding back. Your sister should as well.

That's like asking a penguin not to parade around in his tuxedo.

She laughed in my head, which was perhaps one of the strangest experiences thus far. *That I don't doubt.*

Dez didn't have class with her, much to her complaint, so how did Professor Bladecroft know about her?

Reputations precede some students. Your father's pursuits were well known in our circles, as were your sister's involvement in some of the hunting trips.

I cleared my throat as we continued walking back into the building, trying to act casual, like I wasn't having an involved silent conversation. It was harder than one might think.

I'd like to train you and Dez privately.

I stopped. *Wait. What?*

Keep walking.

I regained my footing and approached the entrance. *Why?*

Her chest rose and fell, and I sensed she was searching for the correct phrasing that would answer my question but wouldn't freak me out. Too late for that.

I want you both to be ready.

Ready for what?

Just be ready, she replied and removed her hand from mine. "I will be in touch."

Unsure if I should verbalize a response, I decided to nod, albeit numbly, and continued walking down the hall to my room. Was I more than a little freaked out? Hell yes.

"Hey, Cyn, wait up," Red called after me.

I ignored her and accelerated into vamp-speed. After Bladecroft's conversation and her desire to train Dez and me, I didn't have the mental grounding necessary to ward off Anastasia and her powerful witchy intuition. I plunged my key into the door, heard the locking mechanism click open, and hurried inside, locking the door behind me. My chest heaved as I fought to catch my breath. Panic gripped my throat, making it hard to breathe. My heart beat rapidly. Could vampires have a heart attack?

Dez appeared in front of me. "What's wrong with you?"

I gasped in shock, clutching my chest. "Gods, you scared me. I didn't realize you were here."

She rolled her eyes. "Obviously. I skipped Meditation this morning. Trying to stay away from Jace. But what's wrong? You look like you've just seen a ghost. Now, out with it."

I lifted my hands and pushed her shoulders. "Can I get a minute? I'm dying here."

"You already died."

"Thanks to you."

She returned to her bed and plopped down. "Here we go with this conversation. Again."

I lifted my hands to my nose in prayer position, breathing in and out, trying to calm myself. I called upon each of the elements to further ground me to the space. My feet vibrated as Earth answered. A cool breeze kissed my cheeks as Air appeared. A warm blanket wrapped around my shoulders, announcing Fire's presence. My quartz crystal necklace pulsed with energy, reminding me Water was always with me. A gentle awareness entered at the crown of my head and pressed down upon me, letting me know Spirit was present. I took one, two, three more breaths to fully ground myself in the elements before I dared speak.

"So . . ." I started.

Dez swung her legs over the side of the bed. "I already don't like the direction this conversation is headed."

"Oh, trust me, you are going to love it. Professor Bladecroft wants to train us in private."

She leapt up. "What?!?! Are you serious? Us? Wow. That's awesome. Like seriously awesome. When do we start?"

I rubbed my hands together, trying to create more heat. Fire's blanket hadn't warmed me all the way through yet. "You don't want to know why?"

She shook her head. "No, I just want to know when. I've been dying to get into her class. I thought about spying on you, but this . . ." she started pacing the room with her arms waving around in wide circles, ". . . this is better than I could have imagined."

I sat down on my bed. "I don't understand why you're so excited."

"It's Professor Lara Bladecroft. She is the most well-known, kick-assiest female warrior in the entire world. People would kill for this opportunity."

"Well, maybe if they knew why she wanted to privately train us, they might think differently."

She waved me off as she continued pacing. "Nope, not interested. Super pumped."

"It has to do with Mom and what she told us."

She skidded to a stop, holding up her finger. "Shhhh." She jumped onto the bed with me. For all her grace and beauty, she could make jumping onto the bed an Olympic event. She leaned toward me, keeping her voice deadly quiet. "What?"

"Did Mom mention anything about forces outside of her realm of influence to you when she knocked us out?"

She nodded. "Yeah."

"Bladecroft said she wants us to be ready."

Dez's forehead bunched. It pleased me that she was finally demonstrating some concern. "Ready for what?"

"She didn't say, but I'm guessing it has something to do with Mom."

She clapped her hands together, shrugging her shoulders. "Well, whatever the reason, I can't wait."

"How'd I know you were going to say that? Are you sure we're related?"

In more ways than I could count, my sister and I were complete opposites.

She winked at me. "You know it, baby. Where do you think you got that fine ass from?"

I groaned. I *did* know it.

CHAPTER
THIRTY-ONE

D^{ez}

"KEEP IT TOGETHER. KEEP IT TOGETHER," I chanted to myself on my way to Elemental History. Of course, I had acted like I didn't care why Lara Bladecroft wanted to train us, but that was because I already suspected the reason. Mommy Morrigan had more or less told me to be ready. Dad had spent most of his waking hours outside of his hunting training me. "Be ready," he'd always said. It had become a mantra to me in all my training sessions from the time I was a young child who could barely lift her sword to the warrior-in-waiting I was today.

Professor Goldwell was somehow connected to the underlying threat that the goddesses and evidently a few of the professors knew about, but the question was, *what*. What was the threat?

The Children of the Sun weren't to be trifled with, but

231

they were a human organization who knew about the existence of supernatural creatures and were determined to eliminate them, especially vampires. But they weren't a secret threat. They were well known, somewhat organized, and determined, but really, once a supernatural transitioned, there was little the Children of the Sun could do to stop us. Sure, they knocked off a few below-par supernaturals, but like Darwin's theory, only the strong survived anyway. I didn't weep for the weak. A secret threat did have me a tad on edge, though.

"Hey, Dez," Red shouted as she patted my shoulder. I dropped into a fighting stance before fully realizing who it was. Guess I was more than a tad on edge. More like jumping off a fucking cliff.

She put her hands up. "Whoa, I'm innocent. Well, mostly. The fallen angel I was with last night could vouch that I'm no angel." She elbowed me as she laughed at her own joke. When I didn't respond, she frowned. "What's wrong? You are absolutely ashen."

I cleared my throat, focusing on centering myself and acting like I didn't carry the weight of the world on my shoulders, which was a lie, of course, but yeah, at least I tried. "Nothing. Just distracted."

She shook her head, her little black cauldron swinging back and forth in her hand. "More than distracted. I will respect your privacy because I sense there is something deeper going on, but please know I am always here for you." She looped her free hand through mine and stopped, forcing me to stop too. "You know that, right? I am always here for you. You can trust me. Cynda can too. I will always have your back."

"What about my front?" I winked at her, breaking the tension.

"That's Alyze's domain. I like mine with long Don Johnsons.

"You did not just use an '80s TV reference for a man's dick, did you?"

She grinned and started walking, bringing me along with her. "I might have. Scruffy beard, tight T-shirt, in a blazer? The stuff of dreams."

I snorted. "Might need to modernize that wardrobe."

"Or bring it back. So, what do you think we're learning about in class today?" she asked, changing the subject. She really was a good friend.

"About the persecution of witches throughout history," Professor Salzbury shouted from the chalkboard.

Yes, Silverwood Academy still used chalkboards. Technology didn't work well on campus. It probably had something to do with the stone building shaped like a star, along with the significant amount of ancient human-made and geological formations located on the property. Or the ley lines, since Silverwood Academy and Prison fell directly on them. Or perhaps they used them because chalk was still considered a magickal substance, and there was something magickal about writing words on a board and then erasing them. Take your pick, but probably all of the above.

We took our seats at our desks, which were arranged in a circle, as the rest of the students filed in. Azalea sat directly across from me, realized she couldn't avoid looking at me at least occasionally, and dramatically stomped to another free chair.

"She really dislikes you," Red whispered in my ear.

"Feeling is mutual. I thought you two used to be friends?"

She wagged her finger in the air. "Not friends. We

walked to our first class together, and she treated Cynda like a piece of old gum on the bottom of her shoe.

A growl grumbled deep inside me. "I knew I didn't like her."

"Well, after that incident, I backed off and let her go on her own. I told you, I love you and Cyn."

"Love you too, Red. Love you too."

Azalea's gaze shot to mine as if sensing we were talking about her. Her face scrunched together in a tight point.

"Careful," I mouthed. "It'll stay that way."

"All right," Professor Salzbury said, "let's talk witch persecution history."

"Wish they had all died," Azalea muttered.

I pressed my lips together and bent my body at the waist so I could glare at her. "Excuse me?"

"Is there a problem, Miss Wickershim?"

I leaned back against my seat. "I don't have a problem, but apparently Azalea does."

His green eyes flashed gold before shooting to her. "Azalea, do you wish to share something with the rest of us?"

"N-no," she stuttered. "I didn't say anything."

"Liar," I grunted under my breath.

"Deziree," he warned. "Don't harass the other students."

I lifted my chin. "Excuse me? I don't harass students when it's not deserved, and I don't lie. Azalea said she wished all witches had died. I can't help it if no one else heard it, but my super vamp hearing did. Anyone else?"

Everyone dropped their gaze, refusing to meet my eyes. I looked to Red for support, but she shrugged in apology. "I don't have super hearing."

"Azalea, are these accusations true?"

"No, sir." She shook her head. "I didn't say anything. If anything, I feel more sympathetic for witches after being falsely persecuted."

I shifted to spring up, but Red clamped her hand on my shoulder, and a numbing spell washed over me. I frowned at her. She winked, knowing I'd never report her use of magick without my consent. I stopped fighting and relaxed in my seat.

Professor Salzbury's eyes skimmed over me before asking, "Anyone else have anything they'd like to contribute, or can we get on with the topic of witch persecution?"

"Let's," Red said, releasing my shoulder before carefully placing her small cauldron beneath her seat.

"Okay," he said, returning to the chalkboard with his back to us.

I leaned forward and gave Azalea the I-got-my-eyes-on-you gesture, pointing two fingers at my own eyes.

"Deziree," Salzbury warned as if he had eyes on the back of his head. As a gargoyle, maybe he did. I clamped my mouth shut and stared at the chalkboard and the two words written. "Midwives and Healers." He turned around, his face brightening at the prospect of an intense class debate. "Discuss."

Red straightened in her seat. "With pleasure—aside from the extraordinary number of women hung or burned for being witches for the mere crime of being a woman, which often falls on deaf ears in a society that, even to this day, attempts at every opportunity to exploit women in all matters concerning her own body." She paused, sucking in a breath. "Midwives and healers both hold a close relationship with Earth, Fire, Water, Air, and Spirit. The midwife called to the elements for divine intervention when delivering a baby, whether she realized it or not, and the elements answered, often with a successful birth. But if said midwife failed to deliver a live baby due to circumstances beyond her control, such as fate, stillbirth, or a breeched baby, she was immediately persecuted and called a witch. If the mother died in childbirth or immediately after, the midwife would be called a witch. If she provided the mother white willow bark to chew on for its pain-relieving qualities, or placed crushed lavender blossom around the mother's head to induce relaxation, or used any one of dozens of local herbs to assist in the labor and delivery, she was called a witch. All this crap started going down around the 1500s because some male religious zealot decided that women should suffer in childbirth for the sin of procreation! Bastard didn't even know what the feck pain was," she shrieked, her voice rising because she'd run out of breath, and she was pissed off.

Professor Salzbury beamed at her. Anastasia was a force to be reckoned with, and her knowledge of the persecution of the midwife as a witch rivaled his own. "Well done. That was an eloquent and passionate explanation of the midwife-witch persecution. Anyone want to talk about the healers' plight?"

Red's hand shot up.

"Aside from Anastasia?"

Professor Salzbury looked at me. I could drop my eyes to study the floor, or I could fess up and reveal that I, too, was a history nerd, especially when it came to the persecution of witches and other supernaturals. Most supernaturals existed in secret, living outside the rules of human society. The rogue ones, however, were the ones who provided my father and other Sisters and Brothers a livelihood when they cashed in on the bounty offered.

I could just imagine Lilith or Maeve or Brigit or Rhiannon, or . . . even Mom, scolding me for hiding my brains. Sisters need intelligence and skill. I swallowed when he ran his eyes over the class on his second pass, and the third time, I raised my hand.

He smiled, pleased that someone else had volunteered.

Taking initiative was also a cherished trait of Silver Dagger Sisterhood.

"Healers suffered much the same fate as midwives and often served the dual role in villages. Along the same vein as the white religion prick who believed women should suffer the pain of childbirth for their alleged 'sins,' assholes like him bastardized the use of practical, everyday herbal medicines, even ones as common as dandelion, mugwort, or plantain or as plentiful as mint. These women, often crones, were accused and persecuted for witchcraft before someone could say 'Blessed be.'"

Red snickered at my incorporation of a common witchy greeting in my explanation.

"But they didn't only persecute women who used herbal medicines, it was also women who weren't attractive from their peers' perspectives. Perhaps they had a wart or extra facial hair or some other disfiguration or handicap that prevented them from fitting in with the rest of the village women. They certainly possessed minds of their own, which intimidated the small-dick pricks and their subordinate wives. And if you had a cat, especially a black one, forget it. They were the Devil's pets. Even women who had dogs or talked to animals or were in some way weird, they were hung, burned at the stake, or imprisoned. Most of the students and professors of Silverwood Academy would have been accused of witchcraft, and one or two," I leaned forward to stare at Azalea, who glared back, "would have pointed the finger."

Professor Salzbury shot me a pointed look, complete with raised eyebrow, as if to say, "Don't go there." I rested back in my chair, crossed my arms, and gave him one of my wicked grins that spoke volumes. He visibly relaxed, knowing he wouldn't need to break up a fight. I'd win hands down, but that was beside the point.

"Thank you, Deziree, for adding to the conversation. The persecution of witches rises and falls with the entrance of conservative religious movements at any given time period or region. Indeed, if a woman or a man lived outside societal norms, they were the first persecuted. Then, as they died or hid themselves, the mania spread outward, reaching any man, woman, or child that didn't fit the standards of the time. I'd like to share with you Joan of Arc's burning."

He snapped his fingers and the lights shut off as his oldschool chalkboard flickered to life.

"Now, pay attention and listen to your intuition. Decide for yourselves what happened. Anastasia and Deziree gave excellent explanations, but they only *told* the stories. Now, it's time to show you."

I glanced at Red, who was side-eyeing me. I could tell we wondered the same thing. Was it a movie or a reenactment or something else entirely? I crossed my legs, rested my elbows on my knees, and rested my chin on my fists, both nervous and excited for what Professor Salzbury was about to share with us.

CHAPTER

THIRTY-TWO

C^{yn}

I DID my best to stay away from Canyon, but he kept showing up in the most random places. A few times when I tried tree meditations under the large oak, I'd almost fallen into the trance state, when he called out to me, ripping me from the meditation and back into reality. He proceeded to sit with me, and we fell into easy conversation until I remembered I was supposed to keep my distance, usually triggered when he scratched his neck at the exact location where I bit him, as if inviting me back. My fangs always elongated before I tore myself out of the bloodlust phase and ran away. Thankfully there were a few other ephemerals who offered themselves to me so I could feed off their blood energy, which lessened my bloodlust for Canyon. But it never truly went away.

My bare feet clung to the damp earth as I tiptoed

forward, begging Earth to quiet my footsteps. The evening dew dampened the tops of my feet, and I asked Water to help me proceed unnoticed as well. Fire offered herself to me in the form of the moonlight lighting my path to Rhiannon's herd. Air stood still, which I appreciated, because it meant my scent would go unnoticed by Canyon, and more importantly, I wouldn't smell him and be tempted to visit him instead. He sat cross-legged under the oak tree as if waiting for someone, possibly me, though I never visited the tree at night.

A leaf crunched beneath my foot, and I froze. Canyon's eyes shot to where I stood, almost as if he possessed vampire hearing or sight. I didn't know what he was, if he was anything at all outside of a human, but I knew he wasn't a vampire.

I pressed my lips together, feeling frustration wanting to break out of them. Signaling my presence wouldn't do either of us any good. But why was he always showing up? Did he want to turn into a vampire like his mom? Was that why he kept offering his neck to me?

I didn't even know if I could turn someone into a vampire. Hells, I didn't even know if I was a true Sempiternal or a turned vampire and what the ramifications of that meant. Or even how I could find out? I needed to talk to someone about that.

As soon as that thought occurred to me, a woman materialized in front of me, and not just any woman. Lilith, Queen of the Night, Dark Champion of Women, and Queen of Vampires. She winked at me when my brain processed who I was seeing. She raised a finger to her lips, then wiggled her fingers. A translucent yellow bubble settled over us. Her version of a silencing spell.

"We can talk freely now."

Moonlight cast a shadow across her face, but I could see her knowing smirk all the same. It reminded me so much of my sister it was dizzying.

Lilith's presence mystified me. She hadn't visited since my first few days at Silverwood Academy, and I had learned a lot about her from Professor Salzbury's Elemental History class along with my own research. When in doubt, search Google or hit the library, and in the case of Lilith, I needed actual information, not propaganda, so I found reliable books in the Academy's library. In some cases, Lilith herself had written them. In the beginning, I also didn't realize what the big deal was about talking to any of the goddesses, but evidently Dez and I were special. I guess being the daughters of a goddess qualified one for unique privileges. At least there were some perks.

"You called?" she finally asked when I didn't say anything. The whole tongue-tied thing kept me quiet.

"I didn't, actually." My eyes shot to Canyon under the tree. Her gaze followed mine.

"You're wondering if he wants to become a vampire."

I pressed my lips together, breathing in and out, clearing my mind of clutter.

When I didn't respond, she continued. "You're also wondering if you're a turned vampire or a pure Sempiternal."

I returned my attention to her. "You mean a Sempiternal werewolf hybrid."

She started walking down the path and gestured for me to follow her. "Tribrid, actually, but that conversation is for another day."

I stumbled after her, my mind reeling with possibilities. "Excuse me? Tribrid?"

She wiggled her hands in the air, but no magick came

out. "You aren't going to trick me into telling you. That's not my story to share."

Anger bloomed within me. I'd kept it under control for weeks—since the night I almost killed Canyon, but Lilith was driving me to it. "You can't just drop a bomb like that and not tell me."

She giggled. "Actually, I can do whatever I want." She leaned her head toward me as if wanting to speak in confidence. "I am a goddess, you know."

"I know," I grumbled.

She either didn't pick up on my lackluster response, or she ignored it. "Part of my charge from Morrigan was to keep an eye on you as a child. You fear the darkness inside you."

"I don't."

She placed her hand on my shoulder as we walked down the path, leaving Canyon under the oak tree to himself. "You do. You also used to be afraid of the dark outside, but look at you now, walking by yourself every night to visit Rhiannon's horses."

"No reason to fear the dark when you're a monster."

Her body spun to face me. "You are not a monster, and the faster you realize that, the faster your true training will begin."

Truth bumps ran up my arm. "What do you mean 'true training'? I thought our time at Silverwood Academy was our training."

She turned back to the path. "It is, but there are other forms of training you and Dez will need to undertake."

"Is that why Professor Bladecroft wants to give us private sessions?"

She nodded. "Yes, and others will present themselves as well."

My sore arms and legs twinged, as if reminding me of the toll my present training was taking on my body. I couldn't imagine how they'd feel after some private sessions. Dez would kick my ass and like it. Lara Bladecroft and Dez got off on sweat and physical exertion. I preferred to exercise my brain muscles rather than get derailed with future aches and pains.

"Am I a turned vampire or a Sempiternal?"

She climbed over the old stone wall and waited until I reached the top to answer. "Does it matter?"

I stood up and looked down at her. "Yes, it does."

"Why?"

Frustration rose within me, combining with the anger. "Because I want to know."

"Why?"

My fists clenched, and every muscle in my body tightened. "Because it's important."

"Why?"

I threw back my head, thrust out my chest, splayed my arms and legs, and I roared and roared and roared. I roared until tears ran down my face. Then I roared some more, again, and again, and again, giving all I had until my vision blurred and exhaustion took me.

Child, you do not need to fear what is inside of you. Embrace it. Latch on to it. Nourish it.

I CLUTCHED MY HEAD, my temples pounding. Dried tears pinched the skin of my face. What happened last night? Flashes of me sneaking past Canyon, then I met up with Lilith. It was all Lilith's fault, the way my body felt this morning.

"All her fault," I lamented, pinching my eyes shut so light couldn't penetrate. Lilith had told me to embrace the darkness inside of me as I had embraced the darkness of the night, but what did she know? She wasn't me. She might be able to read my thoughts, but she didn't know or understand the whole of me.

Boots stomped over. I could feel someone staring at me, but I wasn't about to lift my arms from my eyes to face my sister. I didn't have the strength or the stomach for her this morning.

When she didn't greet me with a sarcastic remark and I no longer felt her judgement rolling off her, I slowly removed my arms from my eyes.

"Heard you had a rough night last night," someone said, but it wasn't Dez or even Alyze or Red.

I squinted a single eye open. "Mom?"

She smiled, her eyes watering. "I can't believe you called me Mom."

Happiness rippled off of her, and I cursed myself for not noticing the difference in the energy patterns between Mom and Dez, because there were some fundamental differences. Of course, there were some similarities too, but all in all, they were different.

I carefully pushed myself up, fully opening my eyes. "What are you doing here?"

"Lilith came to visit me after she dropped you off in your room."

Flashes of last night came back to me. Screaming. Crying. And roaring. A lot of roaring. Then nothing.

"Did I pass out?"

Her chest rose and fell. "Something like that."

"She never answered me. She kept dodging my question."

"Why do you think that is?"

I sat straight up, the word "why" triggering me.

"Easy," she whispered, raising her hands slowly, as if gentling a wild horse. "Easy."

I breathed in and out of my nose several times before my chest stopped stampeding. When I finally felt mostly myself, I continued. "She wouldn't tell me if I was a turned vampire or a Sempiternal." Then I remembered her little side comment, and anger rushed through me. "She said I was a tribrid, but she wouldn't tell me what."

Mom's nostrils flared. Lilith had visited her last night after me, but she clearly hadn't shared all the details with her.

If anyone would tell me the truth, it was Morrigan. "What am I, Mom?"

She folded her hands together, her thumbs tapping against each other. "In the grand scheme of things, there is no difference between a Sempiternal or a turned vampire."

"Except for the uncontrollable bloodlust of a turned vampire." At the mere mention of blood, my throat tingled with thirst. My hands wrapped around my throat as if I could calm it down. "That's what I am, aren't I? Shit, I'm a turned vampire."

She shook her head, raising her hands again. "Easy. Sempiternal and turned vampires alike possess most of the same traits."

"Except—"

She snapped her fingers, and my sentence was cut off. "Sempiternals also deal with bloodlust. It matters not in the origin. One must learn to ease her mind, and then she is capable of anything, including overcoming her bloodlust."

"What am I?"

You are Cynda Wickershim, and it is time you embrace your name and your true self in all her forms."

My throat tightened as my frustration grew. Tears streamed down my cheeks. "What. Am. I?"

Her lips pressed together, and she almost looked sympathetic, but I knew better. She knew the truth and was keeping it from me. It wasn't fair. It was cruel, and I should expect nothing less from the woman who abandoned her daughters.

"You need to figure that out."

"Get. Out," I ground out through my clenched jaw.

"Cyn."

"Get. Out," I said louder this time.

"I want to talk to you. Get to know you. Be there for you."

"GET OUT," I screamed, finally finding my voice.

She pressed her lips together, tears filling her eyes. Then she snapped her fingers and disappeared.

"Good riddance," I muttered, and I almost believed it.

CHAPTER
THIRTY-THREE

D^{ez}

I SKIPPED MEDITATION TWICE. Cyn and I agreed we'd keep our distance from the men who intruded on our lives. Of course, I finally recognized that meditative practice fostered a strong mind, so I practiced out in the courtyard with the pagan prayer beads Jace gave me. The stones warmed with my touch as I passed them through my fingers, and as they heated up, my mind wandered to Jace's skilled fingers and how he'd used them in beadwork and on my body. I fell into a euphoric state both times I practiced outside. Thankfully I had cast a protective shield over me. It wasn't a magickal spell—I haven't mastered many of those, but any person who calls upon the elements for protection was offered it. Even if someone walked right by me, they wouldn't see me in a cross-legged meditative state or hear the chanting or the moaning erupting from my mouth.

At the end of my last session, I felt a presence and opened my eyes to see Jace walking across the path, headed straight for me. I blinked, sucked in a breath, and waited, praying that my protective shield held. It did, but he seemed to sense my presence all the same.

"Dez, I know you're there."

Did he?

"You can't avoid me forever."

I could certainly try.

"I mean class. You can't avoid class forever."

Yeah, sure he was talking about class.

"I took an oath to protect you."

I straightened. An oath? What oath?

He ripped his fingers through his silky long hair. My fingers itched to follow them, but I kept them clasped tight on my lap, clutching the prayer beads.

He cursed silently. "Pretend you didn't hear that."

Can't. Heard it loud and clear. Pique my interest, why don't you, you sly, sexy soul?

Who had made him take an oath? He had seen Lilith when she appeared the night Goldwell confronted me. Morrigan had also prowled into my room and sent him away. In both instances I had assumed they'd wiped his memory since he told me goddesses don't hang around mortals often and they probably didn't want him telling everyone that he'd seen them. But maybe not. Maybe he took an oath to one of them or to their male counterpart. As a member of Silver Cloak Brotherhood, he took many oaths, but his confession sounded specifically geared toward me.

I was tempted to break down the barrier and invite him in, but Cyn and I had also sworn oaths to each other that we'd keep our distance, so I would try to. Really try. Though he looked pretty freaking glorious with the glow of sweat on his brow after his yoga session. He always did yoga first, before meditation, whether we did it as a class or he did it on his own. Yoga heated the core, and he heated my core so . . .

No, Dez. We talked about this. Don't do it, girl. Girl, don't do it.

"Fine, you're avoiding me. I get it. I don't like it, but I do want you to come to class. Meditation is fundamental to unleashing your abilities. I also wanted to let you know I found somebody who could help you control your inner beast."

I hadn't had the chance to fill him in that dear old Mom had locked that beast back up until only the Goddess knew when.

"It's just . . ." he ran his fingers through his hair, "I miss you." He sighed, then turned and walked away.

I miss you too, Jace, but it's better this way. For both of us.

THE END

Are you thinking what in seven hells is this sorcery? Don't worry, I got you.
Keep Reading for an excerpt of Vamp AWAKENED

WANT TO READ ABOUT CYN & DEZ'S TIME IN
SILVERWOOD PRISON?
<u>Join KB Anne's Newsletter</u> and get exclusive subscriber only
VAMP DISCOVERED for FREE! Plus, be the FIRST to find out
about new releases from Best-Selling Author, K.B. Anne.

PLUS, receive <u>Newsletter Subscriber</u> Only Bonus Content, insight on Celtic Mythology, Druids, Witches, Werewolves, and Magic, and so much more!

VAMP AWAKENED: SILVER DAGGER SISTERHOOD BOOK 2

CHAPTER
ONE

yn

LIFE BECAME EASIER AS A VAMPIRE. Walking. Seeing. Eating. Even showering. I still hadn't completely embraced my life as a Sempiternal, but at least it made certain aspects of it easier. The sting of a lifetime of disregard from my adoptive parents no longer informed my actions. I no longer worried my every action would lead to disappointment. Of course, I still worried about a lot of things. Becoming a Sempiternal didn't eliminate my anxiety, but at least, I acknowledged it and didn't let it rule me. Mostly. At least, I had a sister who cared about me and a mother, who try as I might to come to terms with, refused to let me out of her sight.

"Caw, caw!"

"Caw, caw!"

"Caw, caw!"

Well, her or one of her sisters, or her three ravens, since

my birth mother was an actual goddess, as were her sisters. Together they created Silverwood Academy, a school for recently turned supernaturals, demonstrating aptitude to perhaps one day join Silver Dagger Sisterhood or Silver Cloak Brotherhood. Well, if they could make it through the academy alive which some days was much harder than others.

A sharp jab to my gut drew me out of my head.

Today, was one of those days.

"Pay attention," my sparring partner, a wolf shifter named Peeta growled.

"You'll pay for that."

"Promises, promises. It's not my fault when you drift into another world without fear of repercussions."

"I am Air." I point to the air symbol on my tank top. "Lilith is my goddess. What did you expect?"

He shook his head. "Just because your element is Air doesn't mean you have to spend all your time in it. Another partner wouldn't have given you a gentle warning shot."

I rubbed my ribs, that were already knitting back together. "You call that gentle?"

He twirled his wood sword like a baton. "I could have knocked you on your ass. An enemy rogue would kill you dead."

Sometimes people just didn't know when to shut up. I rolled back my shoulders and sunk into a crouch, narrowing my eyes at him. I shut off absorbing the beauty of the grove in Wildwood Preserves Bladecroft liked to train in. I ignored the gorgeous blue sky that begged me to stare at it. I closed off my senses, so all I saw and smelled was him.

"Now, you did it."

I kicked my legs into his gut. He flew across the grove hitting an oak tree before crumbling to the forest floor.

He pushed up on his elbows and shook his head. "Where did that come from?

I shrugged my shoulders. "I've got a few tricks up my sleeve."

The private training sessions with Professor Lara Blade-croft, renowned assassin of Silver Dagger Sisterhood and our Weapon Training Instructor had paid off. Dez served as a much more worthy opponent than most of my class-mates, though I'd never admit that to her. Her head was big enough.

He smiled at me, his eyes brightening to a lovely shade of gold—the sign of his wolf, along with his potential future status as alpha. "Evidently. Please forgive the over-sight. Want to grab a bite to eat after class?"

A knot formed in my stomach. The person I really wanted to grab a bite with and not just from his neck, Canyon Goldwell, was the one person I was supposed to stay away from. I could immediately feel my resolve weakening at the mere thought of him and the way he made me feel—cherished, loved, adored...

"Is that smile a yes?" Peeta asked, eagerly appearing in front of me.

Crap. Slipped off into my head again.

Do it. Do it. I imagined Dez chanting in my ear. She wanted me to date other people. Might as well start with a gorgeous, muscular wolf shifter. The sacrifices we must make.

"Okay."

His face lit up. "Okay, I'll pick you up at your room."

"I thought we were grabbing a bite to eat after class."

"We are. Figured you'd want to shower after I kicked your ass," he said, crouching into a fighting position.

"I believe I was the one who just kicked your ass across the courtyard."

"Is that so?" a voice said behind me. Professor Bladecroft stepped up beside me.

Crap. I was supposed to hide my abilities, and here I was, showing off.

Goddess, Dez really was a bad influence. She was the show-off. I was always the student who had no problem letting my friends be at the top. I even let my ex always take the top. He'd get what he wanted and leave me, feeling soiled and unsatisfied wondering what the fuss about sex was all about. Based on Dez's graphic descriptions, I was missing a lot.

Peeta rushed to my aid. "I had it coming to me. I took a cheap shot when she wasn't paying attention."

Professor Bladecroft tilted her head as she studied me with those piercing silvery blue eyes of hers. I swallowed the saliva pooling in my mouth, anticipating what was coming next. As a tactile telepathic, she could lay a single finger on me and speak to me, as well as read my mind. In the beginning, she discussed things with me she didn't want my classmates or anyone else overhear. The last few days, as my abilities broke free of their constraints, she often used her ability to remind me to hide my blossoming skills and growing strength from my classmates.

"Is that so?"

Her stare unnerved me, but Peeta set up the lie so neatly, all I had to do was agree with it.

I nodded, worried my voice would betray me.

"Peeta, in class, be mindful of your sparring partners, especially those with their heads in the clouds."

He bowed. "Yes, ma'am. My apologies Cynda."

Students around us began breaking off from their partners, grabbing their belongings, and heading toward the portal to take us back inside. I backed away from Professor Bladecroft and Peeta.

Let the two of them engage in conversation and leave me out of it for once.

Bladecroft's hand shot out and grabbed my wrist. "Not so fast. Peeta, would you mind if I shared a few words with Cynda before she leaves?"

"Nope. Not at all." He spun on his heel and hurried away, then remembering he asked me out, he turned around. "Cynda, I'll see you in your room in a half hour."

No, you won't. You and I have plans. Make an excuse.

"Sorry Peeta, I just remembered I told Dez we'd study this afternoon."

You are a terrible liar.

I really was. My sister delivered lies like a fine wine, brilliant and smooth without a bitter aftertaste.

Peeta's face fell. "Oh okay, maybe some other time?" he asked hopefully.

"Maybe."

"See you later, Cynda. Bye Professor Bladecroft."

"Bye," we said together. He smiled as he turned back around and disappeared into the portal. When he was gone, Bladecroft tugged me along with her. "Now, let's have that chat."

"Can't wait."

"You might not like what I have to say, but your sister will love it."

I swallowed hard. If Dez liked it, weapons, blood, or sex were involved. And if it combined all three, even better.

WIDE AWAKE: THE GODDESS CHRONICLES BOOK ONE

CHAPTER I
THE PROPHECY

One of love, one of light,
Spring forth from the womb
To guard from the night.

The power to heal. The power of youth.
Their existence to all a living proof.

As immortality weighs,
One shall fall, one shall rise,
To perish from all humankind.

CHAPTER 2
GLITTER FARTING UNICORNS

I lie. I cheat. I steal.

Parents don't trust me with their daughters or their sons.

That desk shoved next to the teacher's desk? Mine.

The hint of smoke in the bathroom when you apply your lip gloss? That's me.

The "inappropriate" language scrawled across the fifty-seven million posters advertising the pep rally? You're welcome.

Did you find my use of color on the drawing depicting the mating habits of Kensey and her boyfriend particularly intriguing?

Good. I'm glad we agree. But don't get too comfortable with that bony ass of yours, because if I find you in my seat at the principal's office, I'll wrap my black-tipped daggers around your designer-label shirt and make you realize that after-school detention for skipping class is the least of your worries.

"*Freak*," you'll mutter to yourself, and you'll be right.

Oh, and by the way, "Skunk Girl?"

One would think the combined efforts of three-quarters of the junior class could serve as one master brain and come up with a nickname a bit more imaginative than "Skunk Girl." Ever hear of Google?

Honestly.

The torture I'm subjected to on a daily basis is un-freak-ing-believable.

"Gigi," Mrs. Kelso whispers, pushing her bowl of fall-themed York Peppermint Patties over to me, "he caught you on film."

I shrug with indifference as I unwrap my orange-foiled mint. It's only a matter of time before they kick me out. The school shouldn't spend so much energy disciplining one troubled youth.

Principal Donahue's door swings open.

Make that two troubled youths.

At Donahue's side stands a shiny new plaything.

Black leather jacket.

Black motorcycle boots.

Ripped jeans.

Tall, muscular body wearing his clothing admirably.

Expulsion becomes the last thing on my mind. For once the rumors are true, and I am front and center to the greatest novelty our school has ever witnessed: the foreign exchange student. Three words packed with the promise of awkward fumblings in janitor's closets without all that pesky long-term commitment business getting in the way.

His steely gray eyes pin me in place like the dead swallowtail butterfly I mounted on cardboard when I was seven. Together we fall into a cheesy '80s movie scene with sunshine beaming on the drool-worthy specimen while unicorns fart glitter rainbows out of their asses. In a long, drawn-out moment, I imagine all the legendary things we can do together.

Until he opens his mouth.

"You're mine," he says in a deep, husky Irish accent.

The surprise of his voice combined with his words turns my brain into a useless pile of shit. I have no doubt that an extraterrestrial being is about to rip through my chest full-on *Alien* style.

This boy—no, this man—glides across the room and out the door, leaving Mrs. Kelso and me staring at each other like mind-blown idiots. And the hammering in my chest makes me think I'm having a heart attack.

"Doris!" Principal Donahue bellows from his doorway, jerking us back into the present. "Get Dr. McCleery on the line—"

I reach for a black-foiled mint, hoping to steady my pounding heart. Why would Donahue need to speak to Uncle Mark anyway?

"—And send in The Delinquent."

Ah, yes. That's my other nickname.

Original, I know.

My heart continues to pound against my rib cage, but it has nothing to do with nerves about being called into the principal's office. No, this chest pain is something different. Something life-threatening. I can only hope that Mrs. Kelso's defibrillator certifications are up to date, because if I die on shag carpeting installed by the lowest bidder it would be a travesty. Fitting, but a travesty.

The mountains of reports teetering at the front corner of Donahue's desk beg me to knock into them. I find nothing more beautiful than sending reams of paper spiraling in a chaotic rhythm to the floor. Well, except for maybe watching the giant of a man pick it all up.

But not today.

Today, foreign encounters of the bizarre kind have thrown off my thirst for small acts of violence and disruption.

"Cigarettes, Gigi?" he says, followed by an exasperated sigh. "You don't even smoke."

I choose not to disagree with him. When I lie my throat burns like the hot coals I almost swallowed at the Fourth of July barbecue involving intoxication, a dare, and a poorly executed circus trick. The cameras in the school don't lie either. And the pack of cigarettes on his desk along with the zebra-print lighter carved with "Gigi" sitting on top of the green folder? Cold, hard evidence.

I shrug. "I like the smell."

His eyebrows melt into his protruding forehead. Small children have gone lost in there, never to return.

"You like the smell of cigarettes?"

And so, begins our daily staring contest. Each of us searching for the missing plate in the other's armor before loosing the final black iron arrow. These battles have gone on for hours. Sometimes days. Often weeks. Neither one of us willing to admit defeat. Neither one of us willing to yield.

That is until today.

The intercom squawks during a particularly intense clash. Donahue narrows his eyes, still glaring at me as he presses the button.

"Yes, Doris?"

"Dr. Donahue, Dr. McCleery is on the line."

The bulging vein in his forehead thrums into action. "Miss Brennan, you and I aren't through with this conversation. Tell Mrs. Kelso to add another ten days of after-school detention to your sentence."

"So, that puts me at five years past my graduation date?"

He ignores my smart retort, more interested in speaking with Uncle Mark instead.

"Hello, Dr. McCleery. Yes, I wanted to talk to you about Breas, your foreign exchange student?"

That's the hunky Irishman's name. Figures.

"He and I have had several differences in opinion. I would appreciate it if you could come in to discuss the matter further."

Stunned into silence, I sit as a delinquent-in-waiting.

Fire alarms have gone off. Food fights have broken out. Angry parents have banged on his door, and still, after one of us claims victory, he always, I mean *always*, begins with his "Make Good Choices" lecture and leads into "This is the last time, young lady. Next stop, Juvie."

But he skips the lecture and doesn't even dismiss me with his trademark off-you-go wave, because he's completely absorbed in his conversation with Uncle Mark.

And speaking of Uncle Mark, why did he fail to mention Breas's arrival last night at dinner or the half dozen other nights last week? Having some stranger live with you seems a pretty important event in one's life, but no. He said nothing. He acted as Principal Donahue is acting now. As if I am invisible. As if Breas's housing situation has nothing to do with me.

And as for that initial attraction I felt?

It vanished the moment he claimed me as his.

I, Gigi Brennan, belong to no one.

About the Author

KB Anne is the bestselling author of multiple series including Vamp Revealed: Silver Dagger Sisterhood, Wide Awake: The Goddess Chronicles, and Throne of Silver: Silver Fae series. KB Anne writes urban fantasy and paranormal romance with fierce females, swoon-worthy, irresistible heroes, and explosive action because everyone needs excitement in their lives.

She lives in Northeast PA with 3 goblins, a task master, two hell hound overlords, and 2 unicorns, but they don't fart glitter.

KB Anne loves to hear from readers and can be reached at Kim@kbanne.com or join her Facebook group, KB Anne Silver Dagger Readers, https://www.facebook.com/groups/1029150567998675

Sign up for her monthly newsletter! Get early access to her books, inside details, and free stuff.

https://mailchi.mp/14f85a3218c6/silverdagger

WANT TO READ ABOUT CYN & DEZ'S TIME IN SILVERWOOD PRISON?

Join KB Anne's Newsletter and get exclusive subscriber only VAMP DISCOVERED for FREE! Plus, be the FIRST to find out about new releases from Best-Selling Author, K.B. Anne. PLUS, receive Newsletter Subscriber Only Bonus Content, insight on Celtic Mythology, Druids, Witches, Werewolves, and Magic, and so much more!

Contact info:

www.KBAnne.com
kim@kbanne.com

facebook.com/KBAnneWrite
twitter.com/KBAnneWrite
instagram.com/KBAnneWrite

ALSO BY KB ANNE

Silver Dagger Sisterhood

Vamp Revealed: Silverwood Academy Book 1

Vamp Awakened: Silverwood Academy Book 2

Vamp Discovered: Silverwood Prison, A Silver Dagger Sisterhood
Novella (only available to newsletter subscribers)

The Goddess Chronicles (COMPLETE)

Wide Awake: The Goddess Chronicles Book 1

Blood Moon: The Goddess Chronicles Book 2

Dark Moon: The Goddess Chronicles Book 3

Shadow Moon: The Goddess Chronicles Book 4

Oak Moon: The Goddess Chronicles Book 5

Storm Moon: The Goddess Chronicles Book 6

The Goddess Chronicles Books 1-3 Boxset

The Goddess Chronicles Books 4-6 Boxset

The Druid Sisters of the Gallicenial Novella (only available to
newsletter subscribers)

The Silver Fae Series (COMPLETE)

Throne of Silver: Silver Fae 1

Silver Fae Hunter: Silver Fae 2

www.ingramcontent.com/pod-product-compliance
Lightning Source LLC
Chambersburg PA
CBHW030118180626
46812CB00002B/464

* 9 7 8 1 9 5 6 9 1 5 1 3 6 *